Epitaph for a Loser

Also by James T. Doyle

Deadly Resurrection

Epitaph for a Loser

James T. Doyle

Walker and Company
New York

Copyright © 1988 by James T. Doyle

First published in the United States of America in 1988 by the Walker Publishing Company, Inc.

Published simultaneously in Canada by Thomas Allen & Son Canada, Limited, Markham, Ontario.

Library of Congress Cataloging-in-Publication Data

Doyle, James T., 1928–
    Eptitaph for a loser.

    I. Title.
PS3554.09744.E65   1988   813'.54   88-10676
ISBN 0-8027-5713-8

Printed in the United States of America
10 9 8 7 6 5 4 3 2 1

TO MUM, WHO WILL READ THIS BOOK, AND
TO DAD, WHO CANNOT,
WITH MY LOVE

1

THE SOUND CAME again. I rolled silently out of bed to the dark floor of my bedroom, taking with me the .45 automatic that always lay on the top of the nightstand.

A second or two passed in waiting, waiting again for that scratching sound outside my window, the one that had awakened me.

There. It came again, a human sound, the grating sound of leather-soled shoes on gravel.

I pumped the top round from the magazine into the gun's firing chamber and crawled away from the window to the foot of the bed. The smooth metal action of the barrel of the gun sounded loud in the nighttime stillness of the house.

The building had four apartments, all on the ground floor. Two faced the street; two faced the alley in the rear. I had rented one of the rear units, wanting six months at the beach during the off-season. It's the best time of the year if you live year-round in Florida—also the cheapest; that's important too. I do okay money-wise, but I never expected to get rich as a private detective, and I haven't.

The sound came again, closer now to the open window. A gravel border with a few shrubs fronted the house, and someone was in the border. In my mind I pictured a man crouching in the shrubs. The questions that bothered me were who and why.

A friend and I had spent Sunday afternoon on the beach, under the hot October sun. She and I had walked back to the apartment, showered the salt and sand and heat from our bodies, and then joined those bodies in slow-building, repeated lovemaking. After that came steaks and wine and gentleness. She left at dusk, and would not have returned. The shoes outside my window, crunching against the gravel in the planted border, did not belong to her.

Neither did the voice.

"Paul," came a hoarse whisper through the open window. "Paul, wake up. It's me, Norm. Norm Colquist."

I stood up, expelled a deep breath I had not realized I was holding, walked to the window, and spoke quietly through the screen and the open glass slats of the jalousie to the shadow on the other side. "That was a dumb trick," I said. "People get killed that way."

"I gotta talk to you."

"You could have rung the doorbell," I pointed out. "Wait'll I put on my robe and some lights."

"No. No lights."

Something in his voice caught my attention. It had been there when he first spoke, but I hadn't noticed. Now I did. It was fear. It registered clearly.

I put on a thin robe and walked from the bedroom through the dinette and into the living room in the dark and opened the front door. He slid along the outside wall of the house and squeezed his shadowy bulk through the door.

"Shut it," he said. "Lock it, Paul." His voice carried a plea in it.

I did what he asked and steered him through the darkness into a chair and got him a beer when he said he was thirsty. I sat in the other chair.

The living room contained two chairs, both with blond wood arms and legs and print upholstery on the seats and backs. There were also two end tables, a coffee table, a television set, and a couch that converted into a bed, all now only black shadows in the darkness. The TV was rented; the rest belonged to the landlord. The remainder of the apartment consisted of a dining ell off the living room, a small kitchen, a bathroom, and one bedroom with a single large

2

closet.

I said, "I didn't hear you drive up."

"I walked. All the way down here from the pink palace up the beach. Must have been ten miles."

It was actually only two from the Don-Ce-Sar Hotel to the place I was renting at Pass-a-Grille.

"What's the matter, Norm?" I asked.

He sat across from me, only a shadow in the darkness. For a moment there was a silence between us. Then, "I got trouble, Paul. Big trouble." Beer gurgled. "Could I have another?"

I went for it and brought one back for myself. The prospect of getting back to bed was fading from my immediate future. "What kind of trouble?" I asked.

He lit a cigarette with hands that shook. I had never seen Norman Colquist shake, and he and I went back a long way. Trouble wasn't something that you associated with Norm. He was still too much a jolly fat kid, looking for a good time.

He liked to party, and he liked to drink, neither of which he did in moderation, but he was an amiable drunk—the life of the party—and always willing to help a friend out of a bind. His biggest vice was gambling. He couldn't seem to stay away from the tracks or the frontons or anyplace else he could place a bet. When I knew him best, he had held his own and paid his debts, and if they can say that about any of us at the end we will have come out even, at least.

I repeated my question. "What's wrong?"

"I went bust," he replied. The end of his cigarette glowed in the dark. "I can't make my payoff. I'm finished, Paul. I took a big hit today."

"You've had bad days before," I told him.

"Not like today," he replied. "It was the football that did it. I can't believe it. I thought I had it knocked."

"How much do you need to cover? A thousand? Two? Three?"

Silence. Then, "Thanks, Paul." The gratitude in his voice

3

was genuine. "Too much." His cigarette glowed once again.

"You're too smart to let it get to be too much," I said.

"Yeah," he said. "Yeah. Smart. That's me." He laughed bitterly. "I went for the whole enchilada today . . . and I missed."

"How much are you short?"

"Fifty-two thousand."

"Fifty-two—," I began. I took in a deep breath. "Nobody can lose that much in one day."

"Last week too. They gave me time to win it back, but it just got worse."

"Who gave you time? Who do you owe?"

"Some people who always collect," he replied. The cigarette hissed out in the bottom of his first empty beer can. "Gimme some whiskey, Paul, will you?"

I went into the tiny kitchen and returned with a glass of whiskey for each of us. "Manny Diaz's mob?" I asked.

Manuel Diaz had run the rackets in Tampa—most of them, at any rate—for at least forty years, maybe longer. Diaz was past eighty now and sick, only a shell of his old self. The word was that a couple of his top lieutenants jockeyed around the old man, waiting for death to take him out of the picture.

"No, not Diaz," he replied, his words sharp-edged. He paused to drink, and coughed as the whiskey went down. "Out-of-town action," he said. He didn't seem to want to talk about it.

"Diaz won't like the competition, not in his own backyard."

"Keep Diaz out of it," he said, his voice sounding harsh. "I got troubles enough as it is. There's guys out there who wear sunglasses in nightclubs and have little bulges under their arms, and they're looking for me." He lit another cigarette, hands still trembling. The light from the blazing match illuminated the dark holes of his eyes.

"What do you have in mind?"

"I got to put some distance between me and the people I

4

owe." The bitter laugh came again. "I got nearly fifteen thou in my bank account and can't get near it. I need traveling money, Paul. Whatever you got here will have to do. That and a ride to Ocala."

"Ocala?" I asked. "What's in Ocala?"

"A bus station," he replied. The end of the cigarette glowed. "I bought a ticket to Mexico City at the airport with my credit card. Anybody coming after me will think I've gone there. Meantime I'm taking the first bus north out of Ocala. I'll hole up until I figure out what to do next."

I thought I had a better plan. "You have fifteen. Give them that on account. You can raise more."

"Yeah. Sure. My furniture's worth maybe a thousand, secondhand." He laughed, no humor in it. "I always liked to keep the green stuff circulating, Pauly. You know that."

"Call in some favors," I said. "You have friends. You can raise it. What about your brother-in-law?" I had been Norm's brother-in-law too, but that was a long time ago. "What about Margaret's husband?"

"Forget it. Talent wouldn't trade yesterday's newspaper to save my ass."

"It's worth a try."

"I gave it a try. I called him twice tonight between seven and eight o'clock. Sonofabitch is in Naples, trying to sign up some rich old woman lives down there—as a client, so he says."

"You told him your problem? All of it?"

"I got down on my hands and knees and begged him to lend me enough to cover what I owe. I said, 'Harold, you name the interest rate.' Know what he said?"

"Tell me."

"He said I got myself into it, and I could get myself out." His bitterness showed through the fear in his voice.

"If he won't help, buy time with what you have. Fifteen thousand is something, at least. You could make a deal to pay off the balance. That's better than running. If you run,

5

it's the same as telling them you're stiffing them."

"Jesus, Paul," he said. "Those bastards don't want fifteen, they want it all. I show up without it, and I go into one of those big cement trucks. They turn it around and around until every bone in your body's broken and even your own mother won't know you. That's what'll happen to me if they find me."

I couldn't convince him they might be reasonable.

"I'm out of time, Paul," he said, his voice husky with desperation. "When I got back to my apartment tonight, two of them were parked out front waiting for me. I drove right on past. They'll wait a long time before I go near that apartment."

I thought it over. "All right, I'll front for you. I'll take you up the beach and rent you a room. I'll talk to your creditors and tell them you mean to pay them everything you owe. Some now, the rest later."

"No way," he said. "I gotta split or wind up dead."

He couldn't see my shrug in the darkness. It was his life. If I were as scared as he seemed to be, maybe I'd make the same decision.

He said, "I need a gun. Can you give me one?"

"Who do you plan to shoot?"

"These guys are pros, Paul. They don't cock around."

"And you expect to outshoot them."

Silence in the darkness. "You don't think I have much of a chance, do you?"

"Not if it comes down to guns," I said. "Let me try to make a deal for you."

"No, I have to leave tonight."

I didn't say anything more. He knew I'd do it if I said I would, and I knew if he wanted me to do it, he'd say so.

When he spoke again, his voice softened. "Margaret made a big mistake letting you get away, Pauly."

"She doesn't think so. She has what she wanted. A calm, orderly life. A solid nine-to-five husband that people don't

6

shoot at. Nice big house in a neighborhood of nice big houses."

"She still thinks about you," said my former brother-in-law.

"I'll bet. Do you want anything to eat?"

He ignored the diversion. "And you still think about her."

I stood up. "Marriage didn't work for your sister and me, Norm. You know that."

"It could have," he replied. "If the two of you had tried harder. If—"

"Shut up," I said, unable to check my sudden anger. "Keep anything you have to say about that to yourself."

I took a deep breath and let it out. No use to blow up at the guy. After all, he'd stuck by me. He didn't have to remind me, but maybe he thought he did.

He said, "Sorry, Paul. I never felt any different about you after the divorce."

"I know."

He didn't say anything more. There wasn't anything more to say. We both remembered well enough his dragging me out of bars at one in the afternoon, pleading with me to sober up before I put on my cop suit and went out on the Tampa streets with the afternoon shift. It hadn't worked often enough to save my badge. He'd tried; he'd tried hard. It just took more convincing than he could manage to get me over the fact that his sister had left me. I never thought she would, I guess, and I never saw it coming, or at least I pretended I hadn't.

I recovered eventually from self-pity and with that came a recovery from the drinking. I recognized it for the childish clamoring for sympathy that it was. It and the dismissal were shaming experiences and I put them behind me—at least I put them behind me the best I could. We don't forget things we've done that we aren't proud of, nor do we forgive ourselves our lapses. We just go on, hoping no one will remind us of the bad, knowing the memories will haunt us anyway.

I said, "I'll get dressed. There's ham and cheese and hard rolls in the fridge. Make us some sandwiches. It's a two-hour drive to Ocala."

I went into the bedroom and dressed in the dark. When I was finished, I stood by the window. I saw nothing outside that shouldn't have been there. In my first week in that place, I'd memorized all the shadows in my field of vision. If someone who didn't belong had been out there, my mind would have noted it. In ten years as a private detective in Tampa, one accumulates enemies. So I take care to know the sounds and the shadows of the night. It's good insurance.

I stood a moment longer. The sweet scent of night-blooming jasmine came through the screen. I would never have rented the place if I had noticed the jasmine planted among the poinsettias and coleus in the gravel border around the house. Jasmine in the cool nights of fall reminded me of her, a reminder I didn't need.

I didn't see Norm much anymore, and when I did we never talked about Margaret. It was an unwritten rule between us, but tonight he had broken it. It was almost as though he wanted to get something settled between us, as though it might be his last chance.

I returned to the living room. He handed me a sandwich and a beer. I said, "You're sure you want it this way?"

"Yeah, I'm sure."

So we left.

He didn't say anything more about his trouble for a long time. The moon had risen, and as we crossed the bay it bathed the bridge and the water in eerie light. We cut across Tampa on 275. I handed him my wallet. "Take what you need."

"Thanks." He went into the wallet and handed it back to me. "I owe you five hundred," he said. "I left you a little over a hundred."

"All I need is gas money until morning," I told him, but he declined to take the other hundred, saying that five would do him until he figured something out.

Interstate 275 joins 75 north of Tampa, and traffic thinned as we left the city behind us.

"If anybody comes looking for me, you haven't seen me, okay?" he said. His voice sounded anxious. "Anybody at all. Even the cops." He paused. "Especially the cops. Anything the cops know, the mob can find out."

"Why the cops? Something you aren't telling me?"

"I'm clean, Paul. For sure, I'm clean. But you never know what the cops will do." He slumped in the seat beside me.

I had a feeling Norm hadn't told me everything that he had on his mind. It was only a vague uneasiness, not enough to warrant a cross-examination. He'd said he was clean. As far as I knew, Norm had never lied to me.

We ate our sandwiches in silence. Afterward I tried to get him to talk, to get his mind off his worries. We had a few laughs together over some good times past but his laughter sounded shallow, a thin film over his apprehension.

As I turned my Chevy off 75 into Ocala, he fell silent, and he said nothing more until I stopped before the bus station.

"Take care of yourself," I said. "Let me know what's going on." I paused for half a second. "If you can."

"Yeah," he said. "If I can." He didn't sound as though he meant it. He put out his hand, and as I took it he said "Thanks" and squeezed my hand hard.

He started to slide out of the car, then stopped and twisted to face me.

"If my sister ever needs help," he said, "take care of her, will you? Don't let that bastard she married hurt her, okay? For old times' sake?"

And then he pushed himself out of the car and walked across the pavement, his heels clicking loudly in the still night air.

2

TWELVE HOURS LATER I was in an interrogation room in police headquarters on Tampa Street. I was being a nice guy, going in right away when they called to say they wanted to see me, trying to maintain good relations with people I had to get along with. I handed over my gun and sat down to wait.

A plainclothes officer who said his name was Shaeffer came in and sat across a plain steel table from me. He placed a yellow pad on the table.

"You're a friend of Norman Colquist?" he asked. I said that I was, and he asked, "When was the last time you saw him?"

"What's this all about?"

He shook his head. "You know how it goes, Broder. I ask the questions. You say the answers. Let's try it again. When was the last time you saw Colquist?"

If I told Shaeffer anything about seeing Norm Colquist on the previous night, I would have to tell him everything. And Norm had asked me to tell no one. Especially not the police.

"A while ago," I replied. "We don't get together as often as we used to."

"Uh-huh," he said, his voice neutral. Shaeffer looked like the TV cop who always gets the girl. Or girls. He had a full head of wavy brown hair, deep-set eyes, and a smoothly tanned face, and he showed good teeth when he grinned at me. A feeling came from some place that Shaeffer wowed the ladies and knew it and liked it and spent a lot of time and money on it. A good-looking cop can have a lot of fun with that hobby. As I said, it was only a feeling I had, but it was strong enough to bank on. He also looked vaguely familiar, but I couldn't place him. "You're sure?" he asked.

"I'm sure. Why don't you ask him?"

"That's the problem. We can't ask him anything. We can't find him. He seems to have left town in a hurry. He dropped his car at the airport and bought a ticket for Mexico City. Only thing is, he didn't get on the plane. Looks like he didn't want anybody following him."

"Maybe he has a clinging girlfriend and had to get away to think things through."

Shaeffer's eyes narrowed. "You know his girlfriend?"

"Not unless it's the same one he had three years ago, which is unlikely. Her name was Patty, I think. It's hard to keep track. Norm doesn't make long-term commitments. At least, he never did before."

"But you figure that he did lately and that's why he left."

"I didn't say that," I replied. "You've jumped to that conclusion yourself. Look," I went on, "I came down here as a favor, because you asked. I don't have to stay."

He raised his eyebrows. "You want to give me some kind of hard time?"

"I wouldn't be here if I wanted to give you a hard time. You could have come looking for me."

"Yeah," he said. "Why don't you have an office, Broder?"

"An office is all outgo and no income. I do my job out on the street, not behind a desk. Now, what's all this about Norm?"

"Where do you think he might head for," Shaeffer asked, "if he was in trouble and had to keep his head down for a while?"

"I don't know."

"Out-of-town friends he might look up? People who might let him sleep over or lend him money?" He paused. "His bank account's intact. He's smart enough not to cash a check or use one of those money machines or anything that

11

could be traced. Maybe you staked him and just forgot."

For an instant I gave him a steady look and told another lie for Norm Colquist. "I haven't seen him in months."

"If you had seen him and lent him getaway money, you might have made a visit to your bank this morning to replenish your cash. Might be interesting to check that out."

"You don't need to check," I told him. "I withdrew five hundred in cash this morning from Barnett Bank. I had a big weekend. What do you want Colquist for?"

"To ask him a few questions."

"About what?"

"Police business, Broder. He's your ex-brother-in-law?" He waited for my grunted agreement before going on. "You'd know about his gambling. We hear he tried GA a couple of years back after he took a big hit. Apparently it didn't take. He couldn't stay away from the action."

GA. Gamblers Anonymous. I looked Shaeffer in the eye. "I don't know anything about that. I can't help you."

"Yeah. I know. You haven't seen him since forever."

He stood up and put one foot up on the room's other chair and leaned across the plain steel table toward me. He said, "Where's Colquist?"

"I don't know."

"Where did he tell you he was going?"

"He didn't."

"When did you see him last?"

"A while ago."

"Last night?"

"Longer ago than that."

"Where's Colquist?"

"I don't know."

And that's the way it went for fifteen or twenty minutes. Finally Shaeffer tired of playing the game. He went out and returned with a gray folder, which he opened and from which he took a square of yellow paper. From the piece of yellow paper he read aloud my address at the beach.

12

"That's a current address?" he wanted to know.

I said it was, and he put the paper back in the folder. "We found that paper in Colquist's car," he said. "I understand that you move around a lot."

"A fair amount," I said. "I don't like getting into a rut."

"As of eight o'clock last night, Colquist didn't know where you were staying. He had to call three or four people to get that beach address."

"You been checking out his calls?"

"That's right. We're talking to everybody who knows him."

"That takes in a lot of territory."

His mouth curled in a cold smile. "We're only partway there. It seems that Colquist was awfully anxious to get in touch with you. We haven't found out yet who gave him your address, but once he got it, I figure that he paid you a visit."

"You figure wrong."

He shook his head. "You're getting yourself in deep, Broder. Get smart. Maybe you didn't figure on cops when you saw Colquist last night."

"I didn't see him last night."

"Listen. I understand how it is with you, believe me. Colquist is a friend of yours. Hell, you were even married to his sister once. Okay, I understand that. But we're the law, not the people he owes."

I looked up and showed him an innocent look. "What people?"

He sighed. "He also made some calls trying to borrow cash, saying he'd taken a bad hit." His face hardened. "What do you know about his girlfriend?"

"Nothing. I've already told you that."

"He didn't mention an Elinor Garcia?"

"No. Who's she?" I was glad of the turn in the conversation because at least now I could start telling the truth. But I still had an uneasy feeling that Norm had left something out. Something important.

13

"A hustler. Called herself a consultant. The resident manager in Colquist's building found her body in Colquist's apartment this morning. She had five bullet holes in her."

A long silence followed Shaeffer's statement. Norm had left something out, all right, a big something. On the other hand, he could have left out the part about the corpse in his apartment because he didn't know about it. He said he had only driven past his place. I really wanted to believe that.

Shaeffer said, "You don't want that kind of trouble, Broder. Accomplice to murder is a tough rap."

He gave me time to think about it by going out of the room. When he returned, ten minutes later, he wanted to know if I had changed my mind about shielding a killer.

I said, "It's time I called my lawyer."

"Why's that? You got something to feel guilty about?"

"Do I get the call?" I insisted.

He sat down across the table from me. "Sure. After you do a little sweating," he said. "Listen, you sonofabitch, when we nail Colquist, I'm coming after you for accomplice to murder. You'll do hard time, Broder."

"I'll worry about that when you convince me that Norm Colquist murdered that woman. And you can't do that, because I know Norm, and I don't believe he could kill anyone."

He stood up and came around behind me, reaching for my wrists.

I said, "What the hell's this for?"

It didn't do me any good to ask. Fighting him would have only made things worse. He braceleted my wrists together, behind the hard steel back of the chair. Then he came around in front of me, lit a cigar, and blew smoke in my face. "Smart-ass," he said.

My eyes watered. "You have the gun?" I asked.

"We'll get it when we get your friend."

"Norm has never had a gun in his hand in his life," I said. "He'd be more apt to shoot himself than somebody else.

14

What about eyewitnesses? Time of death?"

"Between seven and eight last night. And no eyewitnesses. So what? Who else would kill Colquist's girlfriend in Colquist's apartment but Colquist?"

The time element interested me. It had been nearly eleven when Norm arrived at my place. He'd have had plenty of time to kill the woman and make it to Pass-a-Grille, if he had left his apartment by eight. I couldn't rule out Norm as the killer on the evidence, only on what I knew about him.

I said, "He'd have to have a reason."

"Try jealousy," replied Shaeffer. He put the cigar aside in a metal ashtray. "Maybe he finds out she's screwing somebody else. It happens all the time."

He pulled a chair out from the table and climbed up on it and closed the air-conditioning duct in the ceiling. He stepped back down and walked to the door. "I'll leave you alone to think it over, Broder." He smiled. "Make yourself comfortable." He left.

The heat in the room mounted. It felt like a hundred degrees and probably was. Inside my shirt, I perspired heavily.

The air I breathed turned thick and oppressive, made worse by the dead cigar Shaeffer had left behind. I swallowed, trying to relieve the parched feeling in my throat. I wanted water. Thirst tormented me.

My arms and shoulders and back began to ache. I couldn't stretch out my cramped muscles, and the pain grew. It moved around my body and lasted what seemed like a long time. Eventually Shaeffer returned.

"Tell me where Colquist is," he ordered. He didn't sit.

"I don't know."

"If you remember, you can go out for a couple of ice-cold beers and stretch yourself. If you don't, you stay in that chair, in this room." He headed toward the door. He wanted me to know he was leaving me alone again.

"Go to hell, Shaeffer."

15

"You don't want to get tough with me," he said. "That's not smart for a horseshit P.I. who works out of his hip pocket. Pay your taxes last year, Broder?"

"Ask my accountant. He's got all my tax forms for the past seven years. You can find him out on Dale Mabry."

"Got an answer for everything," he said. "Even got a Franklin Street address, Suite A-Five. Except it's nothing but a mail drop and A-Five isn't a suite but a damned box number."

"Sometimes people like to write me letters," I replied. "More professional to have the mail drop; otherwise the post office has to forward my mail. Last year I lived on an island that you could get to only by boat. Hard for them to find me."

"Yeah," he said. "Stick around and sweat awhile. It'll do you good."

He went away again, but my aches stayed and the walls seemed to close in on me and even breathing seemed more difficult.

This time he waited an hour before he came back. "Well?"

I said nothing. He knew I wouldn't, and he knew he couldn't keep me any longer. As it was, the bastards took an hour to find my gun, or so they said when they finally handed it back to me.

I heard nothing more from Shaeffer for three days. On Thursday he called me.

"Colquist has been spotted in Jacksonville," he said. "Two guys came into a barbershop yesterday while he was getting a haircut and asked him to go along with them. He did. I don't think we'll see brother Colquist again. Not alive, at any rate. Word on the street has it that last Sunday night he was looking to raise fast cash to pay off a big gambling debt. It looks like the collection agency caught up to him."

Cold bands squeezed my insides. "You're sure it was him?" My mind didn't want to believe it. There had to be a mistake. They couldn't have caught up with him so soon.

16

"He left his wallet behind in the barber chair. He may have left it behind on purpose, as a lead. It was Colquist, all right. He'd been staying in a motel close to the barbershop. He used the name of Ned Cramer. Motel employees recognized pictures of Norman Colquist without hesitation."

No mistake, then. The people Norm feared had found him. "Do the police in Jacksonville have any leads on the two men?" I asked.

Shaeffer grunted a mirthless laugh. "Only one to see them was the barber. He doesn't remember much because they showed him a gun. They told him to go into the back room, and he went. When he returned, the shop was empty."

"That's all?"

"Not quite. The men who took Colquist wore sunglasses and talked poor English." He paused. "Oh, yeah, they both needed haircuts. The barber noticed that and the gun. Other than that, he doesn't know anything. And he probably likes it that way."

"Yeah," I said. I understood the barber's feelings. I didn't want to think about Norm Colquist either. I didn't want to think about him taking his last ride or about his destination. I remembered his fear on the night he had come to me for help.

"You're off the hook, Broder. The Garcia investigation is over. I can't build a case against a dead man."

"Norm Colquist couldn't kill anybody, Detective Shaeffer. The real killer is still out there."

"You trying to tell me we're not doing our job?"

"I think you ought to keep looking."

Silence. Then, "Don't cross me again, Broder," he warned and hung up.

I put the telephone down slowly. What must have happened after Norm left the barbershop with the two gunmen was all too clear. They would have driven him to a lonely spot and killed him. Quickly, I hoped. They may or may not have disposed of the body. You can never say for certain. Sometimes the victim disappears without a trace. Other times the killers want other deadbeats to know what can happen to them.

It was a long night for me. My mind didn't want to shut down and let sleep come. It wanted to remember the good times Norm and I had shared.

Unquestionably, we had grown apart. We didn't see each other as much, and we didn't know each other as well. People change, and the shared experiences that bind people together have a way of fading as new experiences take their place.

I got out of bed and sat in the darkened living room and drank whiskey, just as Norm and I had done four nights earlier. I cast my mind back over that night, looking for any mistake I had made, something outside the house I hadn't seen, something that hadn't been quite right. Had there been a movement or a shadow out of place? Had I missed something I should have seen? Had I, through carelessness, caused them to find him?

I drank more whiskey. I had pulled myself out of a long period of drinking after my marriage failed, so now when I have a drink I don't worry about being an alcoholic or becoming one. But tonight I wanted alcohol's anesthesia, and I returned to bed only when I thought I had enough to allow sleep to come.

Later, before dawn, alcohol-induced sleep eroded, I awoke and gave myself the same answer that I had earlier. I didn't think I was responsible for his death.

But I could never be sure.

Saturday morning I jogged on the beach, early, in the cool of the day, leaving my towel and T-shirt in a little pile on the sand. The sky overhead was its usual blue, the Gulf of Mexico its usual turquoise, the sand its usual white. I ran close to the lapping water where the gentle surf keeps the sand wet and firm. I was alone except for the sea gulls, which would settle on the sand in colonies and fly away screeching as I approached.

I turned after two miles and headed back down the beach. In the distance I could see a figure standing alone at the water's edge. I closed the distance between us. The solitary figure was a woman. At a quarter of a mile, she looked vaguely familiar. At half that distance, I recognized her.

She saw me coming and turned to face me.

I stopped twenty feet from her. "Hello, Margaret."

She walked toward me. She wore a sleeveless dress with a light sweater pulled around her shoulders and arms. The skirt caressed her legs as she moved. Her figure was fuller than I remembered, but the weight was evenly distributed. She wore her hair shorter than she had before. It remained raven black, like her eyes. Her skin had stayed smooth, unwrinkled, fair. I had always thought that, with shawl and lace and fan, she could have been the main event in a painting entitled something like "Girl in a Spanish Garden," circa 1850. It wasn't such a strange fantasy, at that. Her grandfather had come from Spain as a cigar maker and in his waning years had gone back to the old country for a young wife, Margaret's grandmother. The wife spoke no English, so the grandchildren grew up fluent in Spanish. And Margaret looked the part.

Ten years and two children had not changed her much. A little, I guessed, as she came closer. Lips not so full, tiny lines at the corners of her eyes, eyes themselves more knowing.

She faced me. "Hello, Paul," she said. "I stopped at your cottage. Your naked friend told me I could find you here."

My friend was the same one with whom I had spent Sunday afternoon at the beach. She had returned Friday and stayed overnight. When I left for my run on the beach, she turned over in bed and told me to hurry back. She probably thought it was me at the door.

Margaret added, "She's a little young for you, isn't she? Twenty-three, -four?"

19

"She helps me in and out of the car. In three years you'll know what it's like to be my age." I paused. She had not come to discuss my sex life. "I'm sorry about Norm," I said.

She nodded. "I know you are. You always liked him," she said. "And you always indulged him. Why, Paul? Because he was my brother?"

There was a time when I could almost predict what she wanted me to say. That time had passed. I didn't know what answer she wanted, or even if she wanted an answer. I said nothing.

She went on. "My car is parked on the street. There's something I think you should see." She paused. "If your friend can wait. Is she the same one you took to the islands last year?"

"No. That was my island girl. This one is my beach girl. Are you having me tailed?"

"No. Norm happened to mention it last year. He said he hadn't seen you for a while and decided to look you up."

"He didn't."

"No. He said he respected the privacy of a man shacked up with a blond schoolteacher and a case of scotch on a remote island. He liked to say things like that to me. He thought it would make me angry."

"I'll bet it did, too."

"Heaven forbid." She took a deep breath. "Do you or don't you have time for me?"

"I have time," I replied and told her to wait. I ran into the surf and dove into the still-warm water of the Gulf of Mexico and soaked the sweat from me. I toweled off and put on the dry T-shirt.

We walked together away from the water, through the soft sand farther up the beach, up the small rise to street level. The street runs parallel to the beach, with angle parking along its entire length. Only a few cars were parked there. Hers sat close to the foundation of the old Pass-a-Grille Beach Hotel, long gone now, the victim of one too many

20

storms and the high cost of insurance.

We walked silently to her car. It was a gray Mercury sedan, conservative and restrained, much like Margaret herself, quiet and disciplined, emotions always in check.

She had left the windows down. I folded my towel onto the seat on the passenger side and sat on it. She slid in behind the steering wheel. The morning was still cool, with a gentle breeze. Before us, the Gulf spread out endlessly, and through the open windows of the car you could hear the murmur of the gentle surf washing against the beach.

She handed me an envelope. It was addressed to her. It had been mailed from Jacksonville the previous Wednesday afternoon, the same day the two gunmen who needed haircuts took her brother away with them. The envelope had been slit along the top to open it, and it didn't look as though its flap had been tampered with.

"Go ahead," she said. "Read it."

I pulled two sheets of lined notebook paper out of the envelope, unfolded them, and read:

Dear Sis,

I'm sorry I left without telling you why I had to go, and all I can say now is that I'm in deep trouble. There are people looking for me who will hurt me badly if they catch up to me, but I don't intend that to happen.

I won't go into the details because you can get those from somebody else. I won't say who in this letter because you never know who will read your mail, and I don't want to get him into trouble. But you used to know him well. He knows about the situation I've gotten myself into.

I just wanted to write and tell you I love you so much, and I'm sorry if I have caused you any pain. I know that I have and that you'll cry for me more than I deserve. Don't let anybody know I've written, not even Harold. Nobody at all, unless it's the friend I mentioned above.

21

He already knows everything anyway.

You can blame me for a lot, but not for killing that girl. I've seen the Tampa papers, but believe me when I say I didn't kill her. I don't care who else thinks I did because if worst comes to worst I may be dead soon anyway. But I don't want you to think I did it, and I don't want little Mark and Lil to grow up thinking their uncle was a killer.

I'd give anything to be with you, but I can't.

Love,
Norm

I folded the two sheets and replaced them in the envelope. I looked at her. She was staring straight out through the windshield. I put the envelope on the seat between us.

"Tell me about it, Paul," she said, without taking her eyes away from the sea before us. "It's you he's talking about in that letter, isn't it?"

"He came to my place on Sunday night," I said. I told her about his gambling losses and his inability to pay and his fear.

"Why you?" she said. "Why did he go to you? He could have come to me. Oh, damn, he should have come to me. We could have raised the money. We've done it before."

"He didn't call you at all on Sunday?"

She shook her head in a negative response to my question and clamped her mouth shut. It had taken an effort for her to control her voice. A moment passed while I considered her. She must have held all the grief in. That would be the Margaret I had known.

I let her conquer the moment of emotion and then I said, "He was scared, Margaret." I debated telling her that he had called her husband for help in desperation and that her husband had turned him down. She didn't need to deal with that on top of her grief. Another time, perhaps, if she ever asked again. It didn't seem important, not just then.

I said, "Maybe he thought your husband wouldn't be as generous as you." I paused. "And maybe he didn't want to

22

face your disapproval, not this time."

"Yes," she said, without turning. "And you never disapproved of anything that he did."

"He was what he was. You couldn't change that."

She turned to face me. "Any more than I could change you."

I made no reply, and she turned her steady gaze back to the endless sea. We sat for a moment in silence, as though the last ten years had never existed. We needed only to be together to see why we should always be apart.

She spoke. "Do you think he killed that woman?"

"No. Norm might be guilty of a lot, but not murder."

"That's what I think too," she said. She turned to face me. "Will the police continue to investigate? Will they find out who did kill her?"

"No," I replied again. "They don't have anything to investigate. Their only suspect is dead. They won't close the file, not entirely. Should something come to light next week or next year that bears on the Garcia murder, they might reevaluate the evidence. In the meantime, they have cases that require investigation in order to prosecute. They have to put their resources on those cases."

She took a deep breath and let it out. "Then I want to hire you to keep the case alive," she said. "To clear my brother of suspicion that he killed that woman."

"Norm's dead. Let it alone."

"No," she said, her voice exploding. "I won't let it alone. He was my brother. We didn't get along as well as we should have. I can't do anything about that now, and I can't do anything about people saying gangsters killed him because he couldn't pay his debts. But I don't intend my children to grow up thinking their uncle was a murderer. I have to protect them from that."

Her wallet lay next to Norm's letter on the seat between us. She took out a check and handed it to me. She had already made it out, for three thousand dollars.

She said, "When you need more, tell me."

"Does your husband know about this?"

"Yes," she replied, her voice defiant. "I told him I planned to see you. He was not pleased, but I'm Norm's sole heir, Paul. And what I do with the money he left is my business. That's what it came down to between Harold and me."

She might have thought it was only the money that bothered Talent, but there might have been another reason. He may not have wanted to spend anybody's three thousand on a dead man, but if she had to hire a private dick, anyone would have been preferable to me, her ex-husband. She might not have seen that, but I did, so it was up to me to try preserving the domestic harmony in the Talent family.

I handed the check toward her. She didn't take it, so I put it on the seat between us. I said, "You're wasting your money."

She said, "It's me, isn't it? You want nothing to do with me." She took a deep breath and let it out. "All right, I realize I can't ask you to do this. I have no right."

"You have as much right as anybody," I said. "I'm for hire. That's how I make a buck."

Her eyes searched my face. "It wasn't easy coming to you," she said, "knowing how you felt about me for leaving you."

"You got it wrong, Margaret. I never blamed you. I blamed myself and the uniform I wore. I got rid of the uniform in the only possible way without admitting that your leaving wasn't all your fault. I just didn't like knowing I might have tried harder to look at it from your side of things. We were both wrong, and we were both right. Let's let it go at that."

"All right," she said. "But I won't say I'm sorry I left."

"I never asked you to say you're sorry. Or to come here, either, for that matter."

She looked at the sea again, and I looked at her.

Finally I said, "All right. We've got that settled. I'll give you the name of a good man to work on this for you."

Her eyes came back to mine. "I'd have thought," she said

carefully, "that you'd want to do this for Norm." She made no effort to retrieve her check. Her eyes never left mine. "He always thought he could rely on you, no matter what he asked."

"He didn't think it," I said. "He knew it." I sighed and folded her check and put it into the pocket of my T-shirt. "All right, I'll do what I can. No guarantees."

"I'm not asking for any," she said. "I've stopped asking for guarantees from anybody but myself." She jabbed the key into the ignition.

"What do you know about Norm and Elinor Garcia?" I asked.

"Not much. I met her once. She was attractive. Dark hair, dark eyes, good tan. She came on strong. She said she was a consultant, and I assumed that consultants have to be a little pushy in order to get work."

"Were she and Norm sleeping together?"

She took a deep breath and let it out. "I don't know. Probably, though according to what he told me she was a business associate. She worked with him on several of his deals, helping set up businesses."

"She was probably the sex attraction."

"I supposed so," replied Margaret. She knew as well as I that men exist who would betray the public trust for an afternoon in bed with a woman like Elinor Garcia. And she knew there were women like Elinor Garcia who would provide their bodies to such men, in the hope of getting the inside track on a deal. She knew it, but she preferred to ignore it.

"Do you know of any specific things that Garcia worked on with him?"

"No," Margaret replied. "Norm stopped talking to me about his business several years ago. I wish I could help more, but I know virtually nothing about his business or his relationship with Elinor Garcia."

"All right," I said, "you may know more than you think you do. I'll talk to you again when I know more about Garcia."

25

She nodded her understanding.

"I'll have to talk to your husband, too."

"Yes. I assumed you would."

"Will he like it?"

"No. He won't like it."

"And you don't care."

Her hands tightened on the steering wheel. "I care a great deal," she replied. She turned toward me. "You and I had no children. You don't understand how your life changes when you do. You have to do things, even things you don't want to do." She looked at me in silence for a moment before turning her gaze seaward once more. "I can't explain."

I slid out of the car and shut the door and went around to her side and looked down at her.

"I'll start Monday," I said. "With what the police already know."

3

I WENT BACK to Tampa Street on Monday morning and asked for Shaeffer out front, in the big square entrance hall with all the trophies and ancient wanted posters. I marched up to the long counter with the thick plexiglass shield that divides the public from the cops and announced who I was and what I wanted. I didn't expect he'd be glad to see me, but I figured he owed me something for the treatment he had dealt out to me on my last visit. It seemed to me he should have appreciated my showing up without my lawyer.

He didn't. We went to an interrogation room and sat down. He said, "I didn't expect to see you back here so soon."

"I have a client who isn't satisfied that Norman Colquist shot Elinor Garcia."

He shook his head. "What a crud way to make a living," he said. "To go out and find somebody with a few bucks who'll fork it over to get in on a little excitement." He paused and gave me a steady glance. "Who is it, Broder?"

"Uh-uh. That's not something I have to reveal."

"It is," he replied, "if you want any cooperation around here." He held a pencil poised over a long yellow pad.

"This is a public building, and you are a public servant," I reminded him. He only smiled, coldly, while he continued holding the pencil over the pad. "All right," I said, conceding the point. "My client is Colquist's sister. Her name is now Margaret Talent. She's married to a man named Harold Talent. He operates an accounting firm in the city."

He made notes. "Yeah," he said. "You see, that's what I mean. They probably have a few bucks. What'd you do,

27

Broder? Call the poor woman up and tell her you could clear her dead brother's name—for a price?"

"No," I replied.

He gave me a quick look. "No? That's it? Just no?"

"Would an explanation change your opinion of how I do business? I have one, if it's necessary."

"I'll bet you do," he said. "What do you want here?"

"Information," I replied. "You guys had three days to work on the Garcia murder before you heard about the two gunnies taking Colquist out of the barbershop. You can get a lot done in three days, if things go right."

He didn't deny it. "And now you want it."

"Just the highlights," I said. "It'll save me a lot of time and a lot of legwork."

"You must come equipped with brass balls, Broder, to waltz in here asking for help from us after the crap I got from you the other day."

"I thought we came out even."

He said, "You want to make a complaint, go make it."

"Forget it," I said. "The Garcia case is in the inactive file, because you think her killer's body will turn up in a week or two and you haven't the resources you need to bring all the live killers to trial. Okay, I understand that. But Colquist's sister doesn't see it that way, and you have to admit there *is* some room for doubt."

"No. No room for doubt. Let me tell you how it is, Broder. Your client's husband came to see me after he found out you were trying to shake down his wife."

"Harold Talent?"

"The same. He says you're playing on her grief. Wanted to know what the Police Department would do in a situation like that. I think he wanted me to arrest you."

"And you told him you couldn't."

"Right. But I could see his point. He just wants his wife let alone. He asked me to convince you that you're wasting your time. What the hell can I say? Elinor Garcia was shot

28

in Colquist's apartment. They were lovers. Nobody else was seen going in or out of there. He ran. What more do you want?"

"Had she been raped?" I asked. "Molested in any way?"

"If you don't count the five bullets," he said dryly, "no. She was fully dressed. Not even her lipstick had been smeared before she fell, as best we know."

"What about her purse? Her jewelry?"

"Untouched. Cash and credit cards apparently all there. She wore a dinner ring on each hand, earrings, and two gold chains. Figuring a hundred and fifty for each item, her jewelry would be worth seven-fifty, maybe eight hundred."

"Enough worth taking," I observed. "What about the apartment?"

"You mean like did she walk in on somebody burglaring the place? No. No sex crime, no robbery, no being in the wrong place at the wrong time. She was killed because of what she had done or would do, or because of what she knew about whoever pulled the trigger."

"What was she doing in Colquist's apartment?"

"Who the hell cares? Drop it, Broder. The Garcia case is closed."

"Not to me, it isn't."

Shaeffer took out a cigar, looked at it, sniffed along it, clipped the end of it, put it in his mouth, and lit it. He let out a cloud of smoke and grinned a girl-getting grin.

"You and I go back a long time, Broder."

"We do?"

"Oh, yeah. I'm surprised you don't remember me."

I tried to call up any memories associated with the face or the name. He still looked familiar and was about the age of cops who'd been on the force when I was, but no recollection would come. Too many years had passed. "No," I replied. "I don't remember you."

He puffed with contentment. "Well, I remember you. Boy howdy, do I ever." He laughed. "You saved my life once."

29

I looked at him more closely, thinking I ought to remember someone whose life I had saved. He saw the puzzled expression on my face and laughed.

He said, "I was up to be your partner. You went to the shift sergeant about it. As I hear it, you told him lies about me, stuff having to do with where I got the money to buy a Corvette. Yeah," he went on between puffs, "I didn't remember you either at first. Then it came back to me. You didn't want me, wanted that redneck kid instead. What'd they used to call him? The Mick? Yeah, that was it. The Mick."

I felt a cold spot in my stomach. "That was a long time ago," I said. "It's got nothing to do with now."

"That's right," said Shaeffer. "But I brought it up because now I'm going to do *you* a favor. I'm going to tell you nothing about Garcia. That way maybe you won't get in the way of people."

"What people?"

He dragged on his cigar and let smoke out toward the vent in the ceiling. "Garcia had uncles, cousins, nephews. I understand some of them are pretty tough boys. One of the cousins has been known to run errands for the Diaz bunch. Those people might not like you digging up a lot of stuff on her."

"You're telling me to stay away from the case. What are you afraid of, Shaeffer? That I'll make you look bad?"

He took his cigar out of his mouth and looked steadily at me from across the table that separated us. "I could show the file on my investigation to any law enforcement officer in the state. Anybody'd back me up on Colquist as the guilty party."

"Based on the material in the file."

"That's right."

"What about the stuff that isn't in there?"

His eyes narrowed. "You saying I have reason for keeping something out of the file?"

"No. What I'm saying is this: I want to know the ground

you've already covered. After that, I'll go out and cover new ground, the ground left uncovered because you thought the case was finished."

"The case *is* finished, Broder. And so are you." He puffed contentedly. "Look at it this way. You got a client, and she's paid you good money. So what you do now is tell her that the cops know all there is to know. Keep some of the money and give the rest back. Easy pickings, Broder, if you don't get greedy."

"Suppose Norm Colquist didn't kill Garcia?"

"It won't make any difference one way or the other to him. Not now. Unless you figure those two men in the barbershop only wanted to take him to Disney World."

"But if he didn't, there's a killer walking around the streets of Tampa."

"Shit, Broder, there's lots of killers walking around the streets—of Tampa and Miami and Philadelphia and everywhere. What's one more?"

"He—or she—is the one I care about."

Shaeffer took the cigar out of his face and held it clamped between the index and middle finger of his right hand and stared. "Are you just stupid or are you *trying* to give me a hard time?"

"Norm Colquist didn't kill that girl," I replied. "I intend to give you whatever will convince you to open the case again. I am ready to cooperate. I would think you would want that."

"Beat it, Broder. There's nothing here for a shakedown artist. And stay away from Mr. and Mrs. Talent."

"You won't give me what you have on Garcia?"

Shaeffer stood up. "I wouldn't give you the sweat off my balls." He smiled without meaning it and walked to the door and held it open for me to go through.

So I went, wondering what Detective Shaeffer would have said to me had he known where my next stop would be

When I left the Tampa Street headquarters I drove downtown, parked the Chevy near the City Center, and fed quarters into the parking meter. I wanted to see Harold Talent, and his office was the best place for that. More businesslike than a bar, for me. Less threatening perhaps than his home and hearth would have been, for him.

I called ahead and told his secretary my name, that I was a private detective, and that I wanted to ask Mr. Talent a few questions about his missing, and presumed dead, brother-in-law. She went away from the telephone for a few minutes. When she came back, she said Mr. Talent would be expecting me.

Talent had his office on the twenty-eighth floor of a smoked-glass and aluminum building. On the door of his suite a carved-wood sign said only HAROLD TALENT ACCOUNTING. I pulled the door open and walked in on neutral carpet, not too thick. It was, after all, an office, not a bordello. Inside, the furniture was stainless steel and smoked glass and Naugahyde. On the walls hung certificates attesting to Talent's competence, achievements, and civic responsibilities.

I told the secretary who I was, and she stood up and smiled and said, "He's expecting you," and I smiled and said, "Yes," and she smiled and led the way to a closed door.

She opened it, and we both kept right on smiling.

Talent stood behind his desk, hip to hip with a young woman fifteen years younger than he was. They both had their heads bent to examine a stack of computer printouts. Talent was pointing to the figures with his right hand. His left arm wound around the woman's back and his hand clasped her upper arm as though he needed to keep her from fleeing, either from him or from the computer printout.

They both looked up quickly as the secretary and I stood there in the open doorway. Talent dropped his hand from the woman's arm, and she bounced a yard away, as though on a spring.

32

His secretary stopped smiling and stammered my name and her excuse for not announcing our entry. "You"— she gulped " . . . were expecting him."

He didn't like it, but he kept his cool. He scooped up the printout and shoved it into the young woman's arms and said, "Later, Diane."

Diane was well put together, and she had selected her pants and blouse to fit so that everyone knew it. But she hadn't her boss's poise. She fled out a side door, her face red and her eyes averted. I guess she didn't see that I was still smiling, not knowing what else to do.

Talent's secretary contemplated the fleeing Diane with frosty eyes while the secretary herself backed out of the room.

Talent's office had the same hard, cold look of the outside room. Even the picture frames were of steel. The pictures themselves showed stark scenes done in line drawings, as though their owner's view of life had room only for the essentials.

The owner himself looked me over for a brief moment and said, "Mr. Broder."

I said, "Mr. Talent."

We had never met, so those few words served as our introduction to each other. I guessed Talent to be forty, maybe a year or two past. His hair had grown thin on top, so thin you could see through it to his scalp. The features of his smooth-shaven face were even and forgettable. He wore a dark gray suit, light gray shirt, dark blue tie. He looked like a solid, prosperous accountant, which I supposed was what he was. I don't know why I had expected anything else or even *if* I had expected anything else.

At least he didn't put on his Chamber of Commerce greeting act. He buttoned his jacket over the beginning of a paunch and suggested that I sit down.

When I did, he pulled his chair up to his desk and sat in it. He stared at me for the time it took him to haul in a deep

33

breath. After that he picked up a pencil from his desk and held it between his two hands and looked at it as he spoke.

"I am prepared to offer you," he said, "a generous quit fee, one quarter of what Margaret has paid you, if you return her check and drop the case."

"Whatever arrangements you two make between yourselves are fine with me. I will accept your check and return hers and call it quits"—I paused to see him look up, a pleased expression on his face, and added —"if my client wants me to."

"I speak for her."

I nodded toward the phone. "Her verbal okay is all I need."

"Dammit, Broder, I'm her husband."

I felt like telling him that unless Margaret had changed she could be stubborn as hell, especially when it came to somebody else making her decisions for her. But you don't tell a man like Harold Talent how well you know his wife unless you want to annoy him, to put the knife in and twist it, so to speak. If he had trouble dealing with me as Margaret's first husband, I didn't want to make it more difficult for him. What I wanted was what he knew, if anything, about Norm and the dead woman.

"Welcome to the waning twentieth century, Mr. Talent," I said. "Your wife, not you, is my client. Her well-being may be your concern, but you do not speak for her."

He stared at me and then up at the ceiling and then back to me. He said, "My secretary informs me that you wanted to ask me some questions about my wife's late brother. Is that still your intention?"

"That's right. I see no reason why I shouldn't."

"Even in view of my disapproval of this course of action?"

"Why do you disapprove? Because you think that Norm shot Elinor Garcia?"

"My opinion on that is immaterial," he replied, pausing for a moment. "Let's be candid with each other, Mr.

34

Broder."

"Whenever anyone tells me that," I said, "the next thing they usually tell me is that they don't like me."

He pushed that away with a shake of his head. "It has nothing to do with you or me."

"Nor with Norm Colquist."

"I had no use for Margaret's brother when he was alive. It would be sheer hypocrisy now to pretend otherwise."

I said, "All right. If your problem has nothing to do with Norm, what does it have to do with?"

"I'm concerned about my wife," he replied. "She should deal with her grief and put it behind her. Hiring you to dredge up more of his involvement with that unfortunate Garcia woman will only prolong the agony."

"She thinks she has to do this for him. If she doesn't give it a shot, it may cause her more remorse in the future."

"I see," he said. He looked upward, into some interior space where his thoughts waited for him. After a moment, his eyes came back to me. "I'm sure you think you have her best interests uppermost in your mind. But I must remind you, Mr. Broder, that I am her husband now."

"I'm glad that's settled," I said and extracted from my inside jacket pocket a worn notebook I seldom use but always carry. I prefer to rely on my memory, which is pretty good. It's also better, when you're trying to get information out of someone, not to make a big deal about writing it down. But a notebook is a great prop when you want to convince somebody you've got the goods on him. It also comes in handy to get back to business when the conversation strays.

I got out my pencil and shifted my butt on the Naugahyde and flipped a few blank pages in the notebook and said, "Now, you were in Naples at the time of the murder. Right?"

He stared at me for a long time with hard eyes. "What I'm telling you, Broder, is that I want you off the case. And I'll pay to get you off."

I returned the notebook and pencil to my pocket. "I don't

take payoffs, Talent. It's bad business. The word gets around. Clients become very nervous trying to do business with someone who's always open to the next offer."

"Make an exception in this situation. For Margaret."

"I don't make exceptions. Not for anybody. If she wants me off the case, she can fire me."

"I undertake to speak for her."

"I thought we covered that already. Nobody speaks for her except her."

He stared at me for a long moment. "Why you?" he asked. "Why did she go to you?"

I shrugged. "I can think of two reasons. First, I'm probably the only private detective she knows. Second, she's smart. She knows I'd do for Norm for nothing what no amount of money would get a stranger to do for him."

"He was a fool."

"Yes, you said you didn't like him. It went both ways."

He smiled a wintry smile. "When she dumped you, he didn't."

"That's right. Norm got around a lot, learned things."

Talent continued to smile without warmth. "About a young stockbroker out of Chicago. He'd have told you about that."

"As a matter of fact, he did."

The smile faded. "Yes. I was in trouble once. Where I came from, Broder, there was never enough. Then I learned some people had too much. I knew people who went to jail for trying to get their share. I wanted a legal way of getting mine."

"As Norm told me, you were pushing a beer company stock to your clients," I said.

"Yes. The company had excellent prospects."

"Sure it did, as long as you gave them a boost by applying a rose-tinted magnifying glass to the profit expectations."

He gave me that cold smile again. "The company's stock went from twelve to forty-three in nine months. Those who bought near the low end, and sold near the high, tripled their money."

"And you tripled yours five or six times on the way up, by trading in the stock's options. You touted the stock, and every time it rose to the next exercise price, you sold the call you'd bought. Some people lost their asses when the bubble burst. Not you. You held the pin. Is that about right?"

"Close," Talent replied. "The details are immaterial. It was a youthful effort, crude but effective."

"Your problem was you'd done your trading out of a fictitious account. When the brokerage firm discovered what was going on, they sat on the money."

"Greed, Broder, sheer greed. They fired me and kept the money to satisfy their irate customers. I let them get away with it because I was young and scared. I know better than to allow people to bluff me now."

"Norm called it poetic justice."

"Margaret was more understanding. She saw how hard I worked to establish a modest accounting practice here in Tampa. She could forgive a youthful mistake. Everybody does, eventually." He smiled again.

I asked the question I'd started with. "You were in Naples the evening Elinor Garcia was shot?"

"That's right. I was attempting to sign a new client. How did you know?"

"Norm told me. He said he called you and begged you for the money to cover his debts. You told him to get lost."

"For you to have known that, you must have seen him afterward. I wonder if the police know that."

"They suspect it. They don't know it. Tell them if you like. That way they'll find out you refused to help him."

"He owed fifty-two thousand, Broder."

"He had fifteen. You could have come up with the rest."

"Would you?"

"I don't have that kind of money, but if I had it, yes."

"Then you're a fool."

"Probably. But a man's life was at stake, Talent. Your wife's brother."

"Because of a hustler."

"You knew her?"

He hesitated before answering, but the hesitation lasted only for a moment. "I met her, yes. He brought her to our home once. His taste was excruciatingly vulgar, especially in women."

"Curious that you should say his life was in jeopardy because of her. Why was that?"

A nerve in his cheek twitched. "I assume it was she who led him astray."

"Did you tell the cops that?"

"I don't remember. Possibly. Possibly not."

"You should have told them. Guy kills girl because she led him astray. Right now Shaeffer's satisfied that Norm killed her, but he needs a motive for the Garcia killing. He doesn't know it yet but he's going to reopen the case, based on information I will provide to him."

"What information?"

"Whatever it was between Elinor Garcia and Norm Colquist," I replied and stood up.

"They're dead. How can you find out what was between them?"

"I don't know," I said. "Not yet, at least. I'm just getting started." I turned and walked to the door.

When I got there, something occurred to me, something unexplained in our conversation. I turned and faced him again.

I said, "You didn't like Norm, and Norm didn't like you. So how come he knew just where you'd be on Sunday evening between seven and eight?"

Talent smiled emptily. "He could have asked his sister."

"Sure, he could have. But he didn't, according to her. She didn't talk to him at all on Sunday." I opened the door and gave him one last long look before I went out. "I might be back, Mr. Talent. When I find out a few more things."

4

ELINOR GARCIA DIED in a ninth-story condo apartment on Bayshore Boulevard, clearly a high-rent district by anyone's standards. Norm's days of scratching a living from the fringes of various business deals had obviously evolved to better things, though he had not had much time to enjoy them.

Margaret Talent stood beside me surveying the living room from just inside the front door. "He bought it about a year and a half ago."

The front wall was mostly glass, tall windows and sliding glass doors to the balcony, but it was covered from wall to wall and from ceiling to floor by damask draperies. Someone had closed those draperies, thus blocking the outside light and turning the interior to gloom and shadows. I shut the front door behind us and put its key in my pocket and crossed the room. I located the drapery cords and jerked them open. Before me lay the blue of Hillsborough Bay and, beyond, the green grass and white roofs of homes on Davis Islands, not exactly the poorhouse either.

I turned back to the interior of the room and saw her staring at the floor, mesmerized. Norm had gone in for a lot of mirrors and geometric wallpaper on the walls and bright green carpet on the floor. Bright green, that is, except for the one large patch of rusty brown near the couch that had caught Margaret's attention. A smaller portion of the carpet in the center of the patch had been neatly cut out, and if you looked closely you could see around it where some of the nap had been shaved away. The whole patch was surrounded by a white chalk outline. The police had finished there and, with their prime suspect gone beyond their reach, had no further use for the place.

Margaret and I had come to prepare Norm's belongings for disposal. She had met me downstairs with the key and a box of plastic trash bags.

"It has to be done," she had said. "And it might as well be you and I who do it."

Now she stood and stared at the blotch on the carpet, at the reminder of what had flowed in Elinor Garcia's veins.

"That won't bring her back," I said.

Margaret took a deep breath and let it out. She had faced the worst the apartment had to offer. That behind her, she turned to me. "Go ahead with whatever it is you do. I'll start on his clothes."

I shook my head. "The police already have all the physical evidence that was here. Sorry, no overlooked clues for the brilliant amateur sleuth to discover and make the cops look like blockheads."

"Then what—"

"We just do what we came to do, and we keep our eyes open."

"What, exactly, are we looking for?"

"I don't know yet. If we're lucky, I'll know it when I see it. *If* I see it."

I went to the short hall leading off the living room and headed for the bathroom, taking the box of plastic trash bags with me. She followed.

"I'll get the stuff out," I said to her. "You decide what you want to do with it."

She pulled two bags from the box. Into one went her dead brother's hair drier, electric shaver, and electric toothbrush. In the other went towels and washcloths and stuff I handed her from the medicine cabinet, including odds and ends of medicines. We emptied the bathroom without finding anything other than what you'd expect to find in somebody's medicine cabinet. What we did not find were downers or uppers or any pills or capsules in bottles without labels, nor did I expect to find any.

We moved on to the single bedroom. I removed the clothes from the closets one item at a time and explored each and every pocket. Margaret packed each item of clothing into the available luggage and, when she ran out of luggage, into plastic bags.

"Salvation Army," she said, meaning the destination of the things to be kept.

We went through the rest of the apartment the same way, item by item. I found nothing that would tell me anything more than I already knew about Norman Colquist. When we finished, plastic bags and suitcases occupied most of the space in the living room.

We were left with his liquor cabinet, partial bottles of gin, vodka, bourbon, and scotch. She looked helplessly at it, as though not being able to decide. I said, "Leave it. The guy downstairs will take care of it."

She nodded. "Anything else?"

I said, "I want to go through his desk."

"Do what you like," she said. "I've had enough for today." Her face looked worn.

I didn't expect to find that Norm had left meticulous records of his various deals. Norm's charm did not lay in his organizational ability. But I also did not expect to find no records at all.

"Did he have an office somewhere?" I asked.

Margaret replied, "No. He used to say he spent all his time in other people's offices. Why?"

I showed her an empty desk drawer.

She looked up from it with a question in her eyes. "Police?"

I slid the drawer shut and stood up. "Maybe."

After that I took the throwaway stuff to the trash room. We left the clothes and small appliances and the furniture for the charity truck. We went downstairs and out into the

42

warmth of the late afternoon. We stood by her car in the shade of the carport roof.

"I'm glad that's done," she said. "But I think I'll wait a few days before I call to ask that they pick up his things." She paused. "There's no hurry, really. I mean..." Her voice trailed off.

I knew what she meant. She hoped her brother would show up, alive and grinning and teasing her. She hoped it was, somehow, all just a bad dream. That Norm had not been heavily in debt to the mob. That gangsters had not abducted him from a barbershop in Jacksonville. That they had, perhaps, only frightened him, not killed him.

Until there was a body, there was always a slender hope. We all have hope, a vision of life as we want it to be. Her vision excluded the nightmare of sudden violent death.

My thoughts went back to a night a dozen years earlier. I was working the night shift with a skinny kid named Mickey Nolan who'd come up from La Belle to be a Tampa cop. The Mick and I picked the wrong night to walk into the wrong alley. Nolan died on the pavement.

Margaret sat with his pregnant wife for the next few days. It was never the same between us after that. The nightmare of sudden death possessed her. And the only way she could put it away from her was by putting me away from her.

Now it had come back. Only it wasn't a nightmare.

She looked up to me. "He's not coming back, is he?"

I said, "Probably not." She had to have that, but I couldn't leave it there. "Norm's turn at bat was short, Margaret, but he gave it all he had."

She nodded. "I'm glad he did." She paused. "Now, at least." She took a deep breath and let it out between barely parted lips. "I wonder if I do—give it all I have, I mean."

"You're doing okay."

Her eyes scanned my face. "Thanks," she said. "And thanks for helping me with Norm's things. I'm glad I had you to do that with." She looked down at the watch on her wrist.

43

It was gold, with little diamonds on the case. She looked up again. "I have to pick up my children at school. Maybe," she added, her face wary, not sure if she should go on, "maybe we could talk sometime. Catch up on things."

"I'd like that, Margaret."

"Earlier in the day," she said, her face relaxing into a small smile. And I said, "Yes."

Something else seemed to occupy her thoughts. I asked her about it.

She said, "Harold called to say that you had come to his office."

"He wasn't particularly happy to see me."

"No, he wasn't. Did you argue?"

"Not really, though there's a clear difference of opinion about my working on the Garcia murder," I told her. "Look, Margaret. I'll try not to rile him any more than necessary so as not to upset your domestic tranquility."

"My marriage is not your concern," she said, her words cracking out, harsh and defensive.

A moment of silence came between us. I broke it. "I'll be moving along." I started back toward the entrance to Norm's building. She was finished there, but I wasn't.

She called my name.

I turned. "Yes?"

She said, "I don't want you two to be enemies."

"I have enough of those already. I'm not looking for more."

She nodded, understanding. "Even if he causes trouble for you with the police?"

I walked back to her. "What did he say to you?"

"That he was a taxpayer and deserved some protection from your harassment."

"Did he say what he plans to do about it?"

"Speak to the police detective in charge of investigating the death of that woman."

"Don't worry about that." I didn't tell her that he already

44

had. My telling her that would sound like an excuse for lack of progress. "That detective is already mad at me. Your husband and he should get along fine together. Detective Shaeffer can assure your husband that I'll get no cooperation out of the police department. So I go elsewhere. Shaeffer isn't the only game in town." I grinned at her, reassuringly.

Her face was solemn. "Be careful, Paul," she said.

I returned to the apartment building and found the resident manager's office. It was closed, so I wandered around and found him at the pool, talking to the guy who did the pool servicing. I took the manager aside, near the corner of the pool where round wide steps went down into the crystal-clear water. Its surface was as unruffled as that of a blue mirror. A faint odor of chlorine rose to my nostrils.

The resident manager was a short and stocky well-tanned man of early middle age. I told him who I was and what I was doing. He didn't want to talk about the murder. He said that Detective Shaeffer had told him not to. He began to arrange aluminum lounge chairs with multicolored plastic webbing into orderly formations around the concrete apron of the pool. I followed him.

I said, "Nothing that you tell me will get back to him. And even if it did, he can't do anything to you."

"Forget it, buddy," he replied.

"Besides," I said, "there's also this." I showed him a twenty-dollar bill from my wallet. "That's for making things easy for me. What did Shaeffer give you for making it tough on me?"

His eyes looked at the twenty and then at me and then back to the twenty, calculating all the while. He put out his hand and took the cash. "A lot of cop bullshit," he said. "What do you want to know?"

"Did anyone see the dead woman come into the building?"

"Woman on the ground floor across the atrium from the

45

elevator said she did."

"What time?"

"She wasn't sure. Said the atrium lights were on, so it must have been near dusk, but it definitely had not come full dark yet."

"How about Colquist? Anyone see him?"

The man shrugged. "Not that I've heard about."

"Anyone else come in? Anybody who doesn't live here?"

"We don't drop the security gate until seven at night. From then until seven in the morning you need a card key to drive into the parking lot. If you're a guest, whoever you visit after seven has to let you in. Cops got a list of five who did."

"What about before seven?"

He shrugged. "You must have seen the sign by the gate. Residents and guests only."

"A sign wouldn't keep a killer out."

"You saying that somebody else besides Colquist could have killed that woman?"

"That's what I'm saying."

The man looked thoughtful. "Yeah," he said. "Well, sure, it could have happened." His face showed he was thinking about the implications. If the killer had been a resident, that was one thing. If the word started going around that a stranger committed the murder, that was something a whole lot different. That could cost money, a lot of money, to beef up security.

"Who found the body?" I asked, bringing him back from his calculations.

"Huh?" he said and blinked. "Me. I found her. Next morning around eight. I didn't need that, I'll tell you." He shivered a little. "Cops say she was shot five times at close range."

"Did anyone hear the shooting?"

He shook his head. "Don't know anybody who admits to it if they did. I overheard one of the cops saying that Colquist probably used a silencer on his gun."

"This list of people who came here as guests of the resi-

46

dents on Sunday evening. Do you have a copy?"

"No, but I can tell you that none of the guests or the people they visited knew the dead woman."

"How do you know that?"

"Because I made it my business to find out, that's how. Anybody mixed up with her I'd remember at the next board meeting." He nodded his head, agreeing with himself. "I don't know what Colquist had going on up there, but if I had known this was going to happen, I'd have put a stop to it."

"Nobody could blame you," I said.

"That's right," he said. "You're darn right."

"Colquist ever give you or anyone else here any trouble?"

"No," he admitted, but clung to the notion that Norm must have been up to no good. "Otherwise, why kill that girl?"

"Uh-huh," I replied. "Is that why you went up to his apartment that morning? To find out if something was going on?"

He hesitated for a moment before replying. "No," he said at last. "Look. I don't know what the hell to think. I liked Colquist. Maybe I just want to think he was some kind of crook because it's easier to explain a murder in my building that way. I don't know."

"So why did you go up there?"

"His brother-in-law called. He said he had been trying to locate Colquist. Said he was worried about him and wanted me to check the apartment to see if he was all right. So I did. Jesus."

I stayed another five minutes, going over much the same ground. He had nothing more to tell me. Elinor Garcia had arrived before seven, apparently. No one knew when the killer had arrived. All the known visitors were accounted for. All had alibis from the residents whom they had visited. None had any opportunity to slip away to Norm Colquist's apartment and pump five slugs into a woman none of them knew.

The only good thing I learned was that no one could place Norm Colquist in his apartment on Sunday evening either.

That he had returned was an assumption on the part of the police, not a fact. Not much, but something.

Of course, Norm could have gone into the building without being seen, but then someone else could have done the same.

"I may be coming back," I said. "Any objections?"

He shrugged. "Not if the sister says it's okay."

"She gave me a key."

"Then it's okay with me. Did she give you the card key for the front gate?"

"It's with the car, and the police impounded the car."

"I'll get you one," he said.

I followed him out of the sunshine into the relative dark of a tiny office furnished with desk and chair. He went to the desk and took a white plastic card from one of the compartments in the side drawer. "Give it back when you're finished with it."

"Thanks," I said and went out.

Elinor Garcia may have died on Bayshore but she had lived in Seminole Heights, in a complex of apartment buildings called Talon's Roost, a name as meaningless as most of the names given to apartment complexes. Talon's Roost boasted a small lake, actually a water collection pond, now required in building developments. That way the developer doesn't cover the whole area with buildings, whose roofs shed the rain directly into the sewers, so it goes to the bay. Instead, the theory goes, at least a portion of the rainwater collects in a pond and eventually seeps down into the aquifer and helps to replenish Florida's shrinking water supply. The developers, who hate the idea of using some of their land for such purposes, have made a virtue of necessity by calling their ponds lakes and advertising lakeside apartments.

I parked on the blacktopped parking lot in a spot marked GUEST and followed the sign that pointed me to the rental office.

The resident manager was a tall blonde around fifty who wore a nice polyester suit over a trim figure. She also wore too much perfume. I told her I was looking for an apartment and fancied one on the lakeside, especially one I heard would soon be vacated, but she was too smart for that line. She acted almost as though she expected someone to show up wanting to look at the murder victim's apartment. And she obviously had no intention of doing me that favor for free.

I dropped the pretense of wanting to rent an apartment and took a twenty from my wallet and showed it to her and told her who I was.

"I want to look at the Garcia apartment," I said, "Because it may tell me something about her that will help to find her killer."

She held out for another twenty but said I could take all the time I needed. Apart from her fondness for the contents of my wallet she was as accommodating as I could want. She took me to the apartment and let me in and left me alone. She had things she had to do, she told me, and headed back to the office.

I took my time. The police had finished with the place and left it reasonably neat. The family had not yet come along to move the dead woman's belongings out. Everything remained essentially as Elinor Garcia had left it on the last day of her life. I supposed the police had kept some things, and I wasn't disappointed.

I found no address book, for example, or any recent checkbook. There was no diary or journal, although I didn't know if that was because the police had taken it or because she hadn't kept one. Nobody had mentioned one, so I supposed it was the latter. Had she kept a diary, it seemed logical to assume Norm's name would have appeared in it, and I would surely have heard about *that* from Shaeffer.

The apartment had a kitchen, two bedrooms, two bathrooms, and a long living room with dining area at the end near the kitchen. Sliding glass doors opened to a balcony that overlooked the lake. She'd spent some money on a decorator for the apartment, and the overall effect told you she wanted her visitors to know she was a successful woman.

I gave each room about five minutes, saving the second bedroom for last. She had it fixed up as a home office, so that room held more interest for me than any of the others.

She organized it well. She kept meticulous income and out-go records, and she kept all her financial papers together, such things as bank statements, canceled checks, receipts, and tax returns. I sat down at her desk and spent twenty minutes on her finances, making notes of people to whom she had written checks in the last month of her life. These I took from her latest canceled checks. The name of her tax preparer came from her most recent tax return. I didn't have access to her address book, so I had to make do as well as I could with the secondary sources.

She also had on her desk a 5-by-8 card file with a couple of hundred cards in it. Each card was devoted to a man or woman whom she had used as a business contact, and each had the name, address, phone number, and family status of the contact, including names of spouses and kids as well as appropriate birthdays and other information Garcia obviously found useful. One guy's card even had his golf handicap on it. The reverse of each card contained data on her last contact with the individual noted: whether the contact had been a phone call made, a lunch eaten, a birthday card sent.

But no juicy stuff. That might have been someplace else, in a safe deposit box, maybe, or maybe she kept it in her head. Wherever she kept it, it looked like it was out of my reach.

What I wound up with were names, lots of names, too many names. When you have too many names, it's as bad as having none at all.

Still, I plodded through them. It took time, a lot of time. I hoped the resident manager wouldn't think I was moving the furniture out. Apparently she didn't, because she didn't come around to check.

Some of the cards had noted on them the words *see file*. The files referred to sat across the room in a nice oak cabinet. This kept me busy, going back and forth.

The stuff Garcia considered worth keeping was in manila folders. Hanging dividers separated the folders. Each divider was labeled with the name of the person.

Nothing overtly giving any of the subjects a motive for murder jumped out at me. There were a lot of newspaper clippings, especially having to do with business incorporations and bankruptcies. Several of the names were familiar, guys who were or had been well placed in the city or county government. I gave the papers in their folders a careful going over, but I could find no evidence of anything crooked, at least nothing too crooked, nothing that would make a suspicious person think that Garcia might have blackmailed one of our upstanding public servants.

There were other recognizable names, of course, like that of Norm Colquist. His folder had been pulled and not replaced, as had that of a man named Raymond Diggs. Diggs I had never heard of, but another familiar name was Harold Talent, whose folder contained one sheet of paper. That paper listed, under the title of clients, a number of business names, obviously the firms to which Talent provided his accounting services. If there was anything strange about Elinor Garcia having a list of Talent's clients, I didn't see it. Knowing stuff like that helped her earn her living, in ways I would never understand. Besides, I suspected she was sleeping with Talent's brother-in-law and had probably learned a lot about Talent by way of pillow talk from Norm.

As for the other file folders, I saw nothing that would give me any kind of promising lead. Still, since it could be my only opportunity to look at her files, I noted down the names of all those on whom she maintained a folder. There were forty-eight of them, all men.

Time began to press in. I returned to her chair behind the

51

desk and sat down and tried to play the recorded messages on her phone answering machine. I had no luck, and I soon saw why: the record cassette had been removed, probably also to police headquarters. I supposed the reason why the box of file cards had not been taken away was because it was too bulky. The police probably put the contents on microfilm, if they cared.

I heard the front door open and supposed the resident manager had returned. I'd spent well over an hour in Elinor Garcia's apartment. Maybe she calculated the value of her permission to search it at a higher figure than I did and had returned for more money.

I stood up and stretched and walked out of the office in the direction of the living room. Two men stood there, just inside the front door. I gave the older man only a brief glance. His younger partner interested me more. He was short and slight of build. He was in his late twenties. He had a mustache and wore a thin beige sport jacket with a pink T-shirt underneath.

What interested me about him was that he pointed his right hand at me, and his right hand held a gun.

5

THE MAN WITH the gun spoke. "Put your gun down, carefully."

I put my hand inside my jacket. I could have come out shooting, but those two didn't look like killers and the fact that they let me get away with my hand being out of sight for an instant proved it. I put my gun on top of Elinor Garcia's television set. "I'm here by permission," I said.

The gunny grinned. "Yeah, I know. Selma called me as soon as she let you in here."

The other guy grunted something in Spanish that I didn't catch. He was bigger and wore blue cotton denims and steel-toed work shoes. He had rough-looking hands, used to lifting and loading. His hard, lined face and gray-tinged hair made him look like he was closing in on fifty, with most of those years spent on the docks.

"I didn't make out all of that," I said.

"He wants to know who you are and what you're doing here."

"The name is Broder, and I'm a private investigator on a job. What's the problem?"

"Problem is you, man. Problem is you messing into Elly's business, saying things about her."

"Not me," I said. "I'm trying to find out who killed her. What about you?"

"We're family, and we're here to tell you to drop whatever it is that you're up to."

"She didn't have any family, except cousins."

"That's us, man."

"I'd think you'd want her killer found."

"He's already found."

"Norman Colquist, you mean?"

"That's right," said the gunny.

"Did you kill him?"

"Somebody did us that favor." He waved the gun a little. "I don't like friends of Colquist, and especially I don't like weirdo friends of his that come here to paw through Elly's underwear to get a cheap thrill."

The big guy scowled and took a step forward. His hands curled into fists. Apparently he didn't like it either, and he looked as though he intended to do something about it. "Yeah," he growled in English. His accent was Ybor City. "Trying to make her out to look like trash."

"You know her better than I do," I replied.

Two pairs of hot Latin eyes stared at me. The gunny said, "You're going to be sorry you said that. Turn around."

He still didn't look like he'd really shoot me, but I don't usually take chances with men who have guns. If you gamble and lose, the defeat is too final. It looked like they planned to work me over. I didn't care for that either, but as long as the gun was pointed in my direction, I could do nothing.

Strong arms took my own arms and held them behind me. It was the big guy. His breath, coming from over my shoulder, smelled like onions and jalapeños and wine. He turned me around to face the little guy.

The little guy put his gun on safety, pushed it into the waistband of his trousers, and moved forward to give me my punishment. He came at me like a boxer, that is, semi-sideways, ready to lead with his left. He planned to teach me a lesson, courtesy of the cousins of Elinor Garcia.

The big guy held my arms pinned behind my back so I couldn't do anything with my own fists. That left only my feet as the weapon of last resort. I let my weight go back on my right leg, and on the man who held me, and aimed a kick with my left foot toward the belly of the guy in front of me. The foot, however, didn't get up that high. Only dancers can kick

54

like that, and I'm no dancer.

My foot caught the little guy on the side of the knee. His leg bent at an angle it wasn't built to bend at. He uttered a yelp of pain and fell to the floor in a twisting, turning motion, holding on to his knee.

The big guy let go of me and hit me at the base of my skull and twisted me around while lights flashed on and off inside my head. His fists gave me a one-two, a heavy blow in the gut followed by one to the side of my face.

The guy could hit. He might have had gray in his hair but he still had dynamite in his fists, which is what a lifetime on the docks will do for you, I guess. I didn't have any time to think about it. His blows drove me back against a bookcase and the edges of the shelves dug into me, helping to hold me up.

The big guy must have thought I needed just a little more to finish me. He wasn't far wrong. My ears buzzed from the two blows that I'd taken to the head, and catching my wind proved elusive after the hit I'd taken in the gut. I had to even things up, and I had to do it in a hurry.

The big guy moved toward me holding his fists low, not worried. He even spared a glance at his cousin on the floor, who was groaning and clutching his sore knee. Looking away was a bad mistake on his part but understandable. He had me up against the bookcase, bloody of face, shaking my head in an effort to clear it and gasping for breath. He couldn't know I had something left. He looked back just in time to see my looping right coming up from the floor toward his crotch.

Just in time to see it. Too late to do anything about it.

My fist hammered his balls, sending them into his groin. He groaned aloud and tried to claw at my arms, doubling over, weaving back and forth, one hand pressed between his legs, the other groping for me.

I took his wrist and turned him around and drove him head first into the wall. His head broke through the drywall between two studs. I repeated the move, this time aiming for the wall where the stud would be. His head connected with the spot I had aimed for. He grunted once and slid to the floor, unconscious.

The other one still lay crouched on the floor. He left off nursing his sore knee when he saw what had happened to his big cousin and realized he was next. He tried to get his gun out of his pants as he saw me coming for him. He pulled it free as I reached him, but he had no time to do anything with it.

I twisted his wrist and the gun dropped with a soft thud on Elinor Garcia's thick carpet. I pulled him to his feet and pushed him against her bookcase and slapped his face hard, back and forth, until his eyes lost their focus. I pushed him into a big chair and retrieved my own gun from the top of the TV and jammed it into his neck under his chin.

I said, "Not even your mother will recognize your face after what this will do to it."

He soaked his trousers. It must have been the wine they had drunk on the way over to the apartment. You could see the wetness in his crotch, staining the fabric of Elinor Garcia's five-hundred-dollar chair. You could also smell the acrid urine stink of him.

His eyes regained their focus and went wide with terror. He tried to talk, maybe to pray, but his fear and the gun pressing upward under his chin prevented it.

I eased back with the gun. He needed to tell me some things. The resident manager had been just a little too cooperative, now that I thought about it. She should not have made it so easy for me to get into Elinor Garcia's apartment and, once I was in, she should not have left me alone. She had known something I didn't know. She couldn't wait to make the telephone call that brought the Garcia cousins. It was almost as though she had been expecting me.

"How did the resident manager know to call you?" I asked.

Terrified eyes stared up at me. He tried to swallow and

nearly gagged. "I called earlier," he said. "I told her somebody might be around, a private dick. Look, I didn't mean
nothing bad. I mean, we didn't want—"

"Just answer my questions, you little sonofabitch, or I'll
blow your brains out. If you're a good little boy, maybe I'll
kill you, or maybe I won't. Depends on my mood."

"Yeah, yeah. Jesus Christ, please don't kill me. Anything,
anything at all. You say."

"How'd you know somebody would be around?"

"A guy told me. Said a private dick was messing with
Elinor, going to make a list of all the guys she screwed."

Nice story, I thought. Guaranteed to get the family mad
at me. A cousin may have claimed Elinor Garcia's virginity
at the age of twelve, but, dead, she'd be considered pure as
the driven snow—in the days before acid rain.

I asked, "What guy?"

"A guy named Max."

"Max what?"

"Just Max. That's all I know."

"Who is he? What is he? Where do I find him?"

He shook his head. "He's nobody, nobody at all. Just a
guy." Max was obviously someone he didn't want to talk
about, which was his tough luck. Like a lot of little punks he
was a big shot as long as held his gun pointed at me. He had
loads of fun then. Now it wasn't so much fun.

I mustered as much evil as I could and put it into a laugh
and pushed the gun barrel into his neck. "Okay," I said. "You
had your chance."

"He works for Tommy Alvera," the little cousin squealed.
"Holy Mother, shit, gimme a break!"

I released some of the pressure. "Alvera?" I said. "Manny
Diaz's enforcer?"

"Yeah. For Christ's sake, don't tell him I told you."

"Keep talking. How did this Max know about me?"

"I don't know," he replied. "Honest to shit, I don't know.
All he said was he had a tip about a private dick and Elinor.

57

Said he was passing it on to me as a favor."

"Why you? What makes you special to one of Manny's boys?"

"They know me. They know I'm okay," he replied. He blinked as a new thought suddenly occurred to him. "Tommy wouldn't like it none if I got hurt."

Shaeffer had told me one of Elinor Garcia's cousins occasionally ran errands for the Diaz organization. "You work for Alvera?" I asked.

"Maybe," he said, caution replacing some of the fear in his voice. "No heavy stuff, though." At that point he must have remembered arriving with a gun. "Look, about what happened earlier. We didn't mean anything. Just scare you off. Nothing like, like . . ." His voice trailed off.

"Nothing like Alvera might do, is that what you mean?" He nodded with convulsive little moves of his head. I went on. "What's Alvera's interest in Elinor Garcia?"

"I don't know. Nothing, I guess."

"Was she tight with Diaz's mob?"

"No. Hell, no. Not Elly. She was clean. She wouldn't touch the rackets with a ten-foot pole. I even gave her a couple chances to meet people who could help her."

"She wouldn't bite?"

"Not at all. Said when she made it to the top, she didn't want a mob connection to come back to haunt her."

"Smart girl."

"She was. She really was. She used to say the only way she'd take anything from Diaz was if he didn't know he was giving it." He paused to look over at his compadre, lying still on the floor.

"Diaz always expects favors to be returned," I said. "Sooner or later. He doesn't care for disloyalty. That's why he has Tommy Alvera working for him."

The little guy looked up, his eyes pleading. "Don't tell about this," he begged.

"Stay in that chair," I told him. I straightened up and

58

walked to the other gun and coaxed it across the rug and under the couch with my foot. The big guy groaned but didn't move. I walked back to the man in the chair.

"Tell me about Elinor. Did she have a boyfriend?"

He shook his head. "I don't know. I mean not as a steady thing. She was getting tight with the guy that killed her. That's all that I know."

"Your cousin spread herself around, I hear. Who else?"

"Look, I don't know. Jesus. I never paid that much attention to what she did, and she sure as hell never talked to me unless she wanted something."

"But you knew about Colquist."

He hesitated. "She happened to mention him."

"When?"

He thought about it. "Couple weeks ago."

"In connection with what?"

"Shit, I don't know. It's been a while."

"Want me to help you remember?"

His eyes, scared, looked into mine. He decided to try harder. "Some deal she had going." He paused long enough to see the answer wasn't enough. He continued, "She wanted to know about some guy that runs some laundromats in town."

"What guy? Talk names to me, friend."

"I don't know, honest to shit I don't."

"She must have told you."

"I don't remember," he pleaded. "All I remember is I didn't know the guy."

"Why'd she ask you?"

He looked scared, too scared to tell the truth. "I don't know. She just did."

I slapped him across the face with the palm of my hand. He whimpered. I said, "You two punks come in here with a gun expecting to work me over, maybe send me to the hospital. Don't cry to me about getting your face slapped."

He looked up at me. "I'm sorry. Please don't hurt me."

59

"Then you'll talk fast and smart, pal. The next time I slap your face, my hand will have this gun in it, and you'll lose half your teeth." I paused to let him think about that. I said, "Now, why did Elinor come to you about this guy?"

He bit his lip and watched my gun hand fearfully. "She . . ." —he breathed heavily—"she wanted to know if he was in with anybody I knew."

"Anybody in the mob, you mean."

"Yeah. Look, I didn't know the guy. I didn't know people on the inside." He swallowed and licked his lips. "I've run some errands. Nothing big."

"You know Tommy Alvera, you said, and his boy Max."

"No, Jesus, believe me. I said to him once, 'Hello, Mr. Alvera,' when he was going into Tampa Stadium, that's all."

"You just wanted him to notice you."

"Yeah," he said, nodding eagerly. "Yeah. Just notice me. I had a girl with me. After he went past us, I told her who he was. I just wanted her to see I knew people, people who counted." He shifted a little in the chair and tugged the wet crotch of his trousers away from his skin.

"If Alvera doesn't know you, why would one of his boys tell you about me?"

He shook his head. "I don't know."

"Are we back to that?"

"No, Jesus. Honest to shit, I don't know. Max just looked me up and gave me the message."

"Who did the message come from? Alvera?"

"No," he replied quickly, too quickly.

"Then who?"

He looked at my belt buckle. "He didn't say."

"I'll look Max up and ask him. I'll ask Max and tell him you fingered him for me."

The Garcia cousin looked up at me, his face losing its color. "No," he breathed. "You don't know . . ." His voice trailed off.

"Yes, I do," I assured him. "I know Tommy Alvera."

60

His mouth worked. "They might kill me."

"Might at that."

He looked away and put the big knuckle of one forefinger into his mouth. "Oh, Jesus," he murmured.

"Or you could tell me where the message came from," I said, "and then I wouldn't have to go to Max."

He looked up at me, saliva at the corners of his mouth. "I don't know for sure, but it was like . . . like he knew it from downtown."

"Downtown?" I went over that in my mind, trying to connect downtown to anything that made sense to me. I looked at him. "The police?"

He nodded. "He didn't come right out and say it, but that's the impression I got. You gotta believe that, Broder. I'm telling it a thousand percent straight."

"All right," I said.

"You won't tell anybody? Nobody so that it could get back to Max?"

"Nobody at all," I assured him.

He closed his eyes and lifted his face, and his lips moved silently. I guess he'd thought that someone would surely kill him, either me or Max, and the release from that fear was worth a small prayer of thanksgiving.

"One more thing," I said. "When the resident manager gets a look at this place, she's going to want to call the cops. You'd better make sure she doesn't. Otherwise, Max will find out from the same people who told him about me that you can't keep your mouth shut."

He sat there, his face white, thanksgiving prayer forgotten, as he watched me walk out of Elinor Garcia's apartment.

I came away from Elinor Garcia's apartment knowing two things. One of those things was that somebody didn't want me investigating Elinor Garcia's murder and thought I could be scared off with a little roughing up. According to the little cousin, the message had come from downtown via somebody named Max, who worked for Tommy Alvera, chief enforcer for the Manny Diaz organization.

Now I could have tried to look up this Max and find out who had put him on to me, but that could get me sidetracked into a confrontation with Alvera, which I didn't need. Besides, I thought I already knew who had tipped them to me, so I headed the Chevy toward Tampa Street and police headquarters and Detective Shaeffer.

The second thing I came out of there with was a name, Raymond Diggs. It wasn't much, but it was my next step after I straightened a few things out with Shaeffer.

I parked in the big lot beside headquarters where the sign said that visitors were limited to four hours' parking. I wondered what they would do with my car if they decided to keep me. Keep me they might, as steamed as I was at Shaeffer.

I went in the side door and applied at the hole in the big plexiglass shield. I said, "Broder to see Detective Shaeffer."

The policewoman went away and came back and said that Shaeffer was out and did I want to see anyone else, and, since I didn't, did I want to leave my name, which I did. Then I left and drove out toward the stadium to a bar that is a bar, not a nightclub or a lounge or anything else, just a bar where you can get booze and beer and great sandwiches.

I've known the bartender for a long time, and I said to him, as I stood up to the bar, "I want to do mayhem on a cop, Jerry."

"Not a good idea," he said. "Drink?"

"Double scotch, water. He set me up, the sonofabitch."

Jerry nodded noncommittally and went for my booze. He brought it back and put it in front of me. "What's going on?" he asked. I told him about the case I was working on and how Shaeffer was stonewalling.

I said, "The last straw was for him to send those two punks to work me over." Jerry shook his head and clucked his sympathy. I took a deep breath and let it out and said, "I'm not

62

going to get anywhere with that sonofabitch. He's made up his mind and that's it. In addition, Talent's leaning on him."

Jerry moved away to serve another customer. By the time he came back, I had an idea. I looked at it front, back, and sideways. It wasn't much of an idea, but it might work. I couldn't do anything about Shaeffer, but Harold Talent didn't wear a badge. Him I could maybe do something about.

I used the pay phone to track down a woman who had helped me before when I needed information from the telephone company. I could have gone higher up, way high up, since I had once saved the hide of a grateful major executive, but this task didn't require that much leverage.

I told my friend, "It's a question of billings to the number of Norman Colquist. He's missing and presumed dead." She knew all about it from the evening news. "Anyway," I continued, explaining that I had been retained by the family with full authority to look into his affairs, "he made two calls to Naples the night he split, both probably billed to his calling card. Can you track those down?"

She called back in an hour. No calls billed to Norm's account. She had a possible explanation that didn't help me a bit. "Quarters," she said. "Maybe he just put quarters into the slot. It still happens, you know."

"Thanks," I said. "Thanks a whole lot." I hung up. I had planned to hold Talent's feet to the fire, only now I had no fire, just a lot of smoke. Well, that would have to do, but only after I had another whiskey followed by a Reuben sandwich, specialty of the house, hot and thick and juicy. Then I'd be ready to call Talent and, I hoped, to bluff him.

He was spending a quiet evening at home, so he said. It had started to rain around six or a little after and continued, on and off. He didn't want to leave the snugness of the Talent hearth, especially not to see me.

"I'm sure I can find your house," I said.

He didn't want that either. What he wanted was for me to get off the telephone and leave him alone. "I have nothing to say to you," he informed me.

"We'll talk about those telephone calls Norm made to you the night Elinor Garcia died. You forgot to tell the police about them. They'd be interested."

"I have nothing further to say to the police."

"To your wife, then. She doesn't know her kid brother begged you for help and you turned him down."

A long silence answered my implied threat. Finally he spoke. "Where will I meet you?"

"There's a McDonald's at West Kennedy and Hesperides. I'll be at the rear of the parking lot, backed in, parking lights on. Don't be long."

6

HE WASN'T. HE pulled in alongside of me, his car about a foot away from mine. He drove a sporty-looking gray Porsche with beads of water from the rain glistening on its metal skin. Made my dirty five-year-old Chevy look like something out of a junkyard auction.

His window slid down smoothly. "What do you want, Broder?"

"For you to go to the police and tell them that Norm was busy calling you in Naples and asking for money at the same time he was supposed to be shooting Elinor Garcia."

"And why should I do that?"

"Because that information would weigh in on the side of having the case reopened, which is what your wife is paying me to get them to do."

"Then why don't you tell them?"

"It wasn't me Norm called. Besides, they would consider the information self-serving, coming from me. With you it's different. You're already on record with the cops over your opposition to starting up the investigation. Shaeffer told me you talked to him."

"Yes, of course," he said. He seemed to think it over. "On the other hand, with that opposition already well known, why should I change my mind?"

"You want to help."

"But I don't."

"But you will."

"Why should I?"

"If you don't, your wife will hear about the calls from me.

She'll know you turned Norm down when he asked for help."

"Your word against mine?" he retorted.

"Right. Want to give it a try?"

The rain had started again, not hard, just enough for it to bounce off the surface of Talent's car in tiny, fractured crystals reflecting the light from the restaurant. I could feel its dampness against my face. Little rivulets ran down the windshield of my car.

Talent thought it over. "I might," he said. "As you pointed out this morning in my office, he could hardly have known where I would be. Margaret would understand that. I would deny that he had called me and use your own argument against you."

I thought I saw, in the uncertain light, a smile come to his face. A car drove by, curving in toward the drive-in window. Its tires splashed water outward.

Time for the bluff. "No good," I said. "There'll be a record of his calls with the telephone company."

He scoffed at the suggestion. "From a pay phone?"

"How do you know he called from a pay phone?"

"He told me, Broder. There'll be no record."

I already knew there was no record. I doubted he would have gone to the trouble to find it out. That's the basis of all the bluffs ever thought up by man: that you know something the other guy doesn't.

"When was the last time you knew Norm Colquist to pay cash for anything except at the track? He'd have used his phone card, and for that there'll be a record."

He sat in silence for a long time, so long I thought I should help him understand the situation.

"It's like this," I explained. "The phone company would charge those calls to Norm's phone. The records will show the date, time, and number called. It's going to be difficult as all hell for you to say those phone calls never occurred, not with that kind of evidence. Furthermore, when the cops check the number called and find out that it was the Ritz-

Carlton or the Registry or whatever and you were registered there, it'll be hard as hell to convince your wife that he was calling anybody but you. You see where that leaves you?"

"Yes," he replied. "I see. Tell me, Mr. Broder. Whose interests do you really have at heart in this matter?"

"My client's," I said, knowing he was playing for time, trying to come up with something to deflect my insistence that he take the story of the phone calls to the police.

"As long as she pays you, you will do what she thinks she wants done. So, as long as she provides your fee, you are happy to feed her illusion of Norman's innocence."

"You're going to the cops with the story of those phone calls, and it makes no difference what you think my motives are."

"We shall never find ourselves comfortable around each other, Broder, but surely we can act in concert where Margaret's well-being is concerned."

"In other words, you and I will decide what's best for her."

"Exactly. You and I can look objectively at the situation, whereas she cannot. Between us we can lead her into the least destructive course of action."

"You have a suggestion to make."

"Yes. Make a pretense of looking into the case. Tell her these things take time. Gradually, as her shock and pain subside, she'll look at the whole tragic mess more calmly. In the meantime, we need to look after her—together."

"Then put her on an airplane to London or Paris. Put both of you on it. But don't ask me to play that game, because I'm the least objective person involved."

He stared at me through the invisible curtain of rain that divided us, not understanding.

I said, "Norm came to me for help. He depended on me. No one—but no one—should have known where he was, but someone did. I have to know how that someone knew, whether it was because I was careless, whether it was me who cost Norm his life. I don't think it was, but I want to know, if

I can, and the first thing is to get the cops to find out who killed that girl and why, and why it was so important for Norm to take the rap for it."

"And for that to happen, you will force me to go to the police and tell them about those telephone calls."

"That's right. Shaeffer pulled the curtain down on the case. You're going to get him to pull it back up again."

"You're wrong," Talent said. "What I would tell him would only make him more certain that Norman was guilty. You wouldn't want me to say that Norman had confessed to me over the telephone, would you?"

Car headlights flashed into my face, backlighting Talent's form, seated only an arm's length from me. The lights, putting his face in deep shadow and washing my eyes with their brightness, hid his expression as effectively as a mask.

I said, "That would sew up the case against Norm."

"Yes," he replied. "I see it that way too. In addition, it would make you a virtual accomplice, in that you helped him flee after the crime. You don't dare tell anyone about those calls because it's an admission that he came to you for help in making his escape." He paused for the space of a breath. "The offer to work together remains open."

"To protect Margaret."

"Of course," he said. His face seemed to smile in the shadows, and the tone of his voice reflected that smile.

"You're awfully anxious to close the file on Norm as Elinor Garcia's murderer. I wonder if there's more to it than concern for your wife."

"You're tired and frustrated," he said. "Failure does that to a man." He was trying hard to keep the smile in his voice. "Unthinking accusations can cause you a great deal of trouble."

"Maybe. I'll apologize if there's nothing to it." I started the car engine. "But I'll never know unless I keep looking, will I?"

Talent was right. I was frustrated. I couldn't deliver him to the police, and I couldn't make him go in on his own. He had called my bluff. Even if I could prove Norm had made those phone calls, Talent would lie and say Norm confessed to having killed Garcia.

"Great," I said to the windshield wipers, methodically brushing away the rain in front of me. "Just great." That way took me farther away from getting Shaeffer to reopen the case or to getting Shaeffer overruled by a superior.

I felt I had to do something, anything, rather than call it a night and head for the beach place. I had to have something to start on the next morning. My worst days are those that begin with no idea of what to do. I needed a start for the next day, so not having anywhere better to look for it I returned to the scene of the crime.

I let myself into Norm's place with the key Margaret had given me. I turned on lights and poured myself a drink from Norm's liquor cabinet, though I had to drink it without ice. Margaret had turned off the icemaker and disconnected the refrigerator. I turned on the stereo and found the quiet music station I liked and called the answering service and told Lori what number I could be reached on. After that I stalked the apartment, drink in hand.

I wasn't sure what I was looking for: inspiration, probably. There wasn't much else. There was little sense of the living Norman Colquist in the space enclosed by those walls and even less of Elinor Garcia, attractive young striver, seeker after fortune with only her brains and her body to take her where she wanted to go.

I made another drink and sat in a big chair in the living room and tried to conjure up the ghosts of the two of them to tell me what had brought them together. Norm's fortunes had noticeably improved since I had last seen him. Possibly that had attracted her to him. With a keen eye on the main chance, Elinor had selected Norm.

Norm? It didn't work for me, not at all. I tried to put aside the feeling we all have about those we knew in earlier days being hardly worthy of great fortunes or great office. But Norm as the vehicle to riches that a hard-charger like Elinor Garcia would tie her star to?

I thought some more about Elinor and Norm. I thought about Harold Talent, too. And I thought about Mrs. Talent. Her I didn't want to think about, not alone and drinking and with the stereo playing quiet music around me. So I dragged my thoughts back to Elinor and Norm. Elinor and Norm. Elinor and Norm. Margaret . . .

The phone woke me. At first I couldn't find it in the unfamiliar surroundings. It rang five times before I snatched it up. "Yes?"

"Broder?" The voice was male and familiar.

I said, "This is Broder."

"Shaeffer. I heard you were looking for me."

"You heard right."

"Okay. I want to see you. Now. Just you and me."

"That suits me. Where?"

"Riverfront Park. Be there in fifteen minutes."

Night enveloped me after I killed my headlights. I had parked a dozen steps away from the other car, a plain dark sedan. I gave my eyes a moment to get accustomed to the darkness before I slid out and walked across the pavement toward the other car.

The man in the dark sedan turned to watch my approach. He spoke through the open window on his side of the car. "Get in."

"No," I said. "Out here. I like the fresh air."

Shaeffer shrugged and pushed himself out of the unmarked police car and joined me at the low wall. Below us the Hillsborough River flowed gently toward the bay, its waters black in the night darkness, giving off shimmering reflections of the city lights across the river. The rain had called it quits, apparently, though any view of the night stars

70

was still blocked by heavy clouds above.

The park around us seemed deserted, empty. Its nighttime population—men wanting quick anonymous sex or shooters looking for a needle—would stay clear of Shaeffer's plain Dodge sedan. They'd figure it to be a setup, that he'd have a half dozen cruisers ready to pounce. Only I knew differently.

"How official is this?" I asked him.

"Semi," he replied. "You can lay off the Garcia thing, Broder. It's all wrapped up." He paused for a brief moment and added, "They've found Colquist. He's dead."

"Who's they? And where?"

"In a drainage ditch off Interstate Ten," he replied. "A Duval county sheriff's deputy found the body."

Something cold and heavy lay inside me, something I had not expected. I had thought, since hearing of Norm's abduction from the Jacksonville barbershop, that I was prepared for the discovery of his body. Now I found out that I wasn't.

"They're sure it's Colquist?" I asked, mindful that he'd left his wallet in the barbershop.

Shaeffer came closer and nodded. "The body was wearing his clothes and his jewelry. What the hell do you think?"

"They'll want a positive I.D. from a family member," I said.

"Yeah," he replied. "The body was in bad shape. Not a nice thing for a loved one to see, but it's got to be done."

I felt a little sick. "I'll do it," I said.

"I hear the sister has a husband, Broder. Don't you figure she'd ask him if she isn't up to it?"

"You've informed the family?"

"That's right. A little while ago. Mr. Talent took me aside and told me you are still making a nuisance of yourself, taking advantage of his wife's grief. I figure there's more to it than that. Something he doesn't want to talk about."

"Which would be what?"

"He doesn't want his wife's ex-husband getting that close to her, maybe renewing old memories, old passions. Fact is, Broder, I wouldn't blame you. Lot of woman there. Problem

71

is, your fun is my headache."

"Talent's leaning on you."

"People don't lean on me, Broder." His voice turned hard. "You better keep that in mind."

"What I have in mind is this. Talent doesn't want this case investigated, for any reason you can dream up. He tells me it's because of his wife's grief. You tell me he's jealous. Maybe it's all of that, and maybe it's more. But what I see is a cop standing on his head for this guy."

When he shook his head, the motion was like the waving of a shadow. "You're a nuisance, Broder. Like having a sore pimple on your ass. Every time you sit down, it reminds you it's there. That's you, a pimple on my ass. And I don't need the aggravation. The Garcia case is closed. Period. Me and everybody else in Homicide have got more than we can handle with pending cases. We don't need you stirring up smoke over a finished case."

"Doesn't it bother you to know that the real killer could still be on the street?"

"It would, if I knew it. But I don't know it. I don't even think it. They found Garcia's killer in a drainage ditch up by Baldwin." He paused. "And they found the gun that killed her with him."

I digested that as Shaeffer took two steps backward and leaned against the fender of his car and folded his arms with satisfaction. My eyes had by then become accustomed to the gloom. The city lights, diffused by the low-lying clouds in the sky, made enough half-light to see him clearly.

"You see, Broder, it's over," he said. "The gun wraps it up. You've got nothing to investigate."

"The gun's a plant."

He straightened up and dropped his arms. "Get smart. Tell Mrs. Talent she's wasting her money. Tell her you're dropping the case."

"But I'm not."

He moved a step closer. "You're going to do it my way,

Broder. Either that or I start putting the squeeze on you."

"When you squeeze a sore pimple, it hurts," I reminded him. "You've been blocking me on this investigation since the start, Shaeffer, and I think I know what you're scared of. If other people start looking over your shoulder at how you work, they may start seeing things you don't want them to see. That's what's got you worried, and it's a big enough worry to bring you down here to the river at night for this private little chat."

"You got it the wrong way around," he said, a warning note coming into his voice. "I'm not worried. You're worried—or you ought to be."

"I've had cops threaten me before, Shaeffer. Good ones and bad ones. The difference is that only bad cops try to bluff. Good night, Detective Shaeffer."

I turned and walked toward my car.

Shaeffer spoke to my back. "I'll put you away, Broder."

I took my gun from my belt holster and put it in my pocket and kept my hand there with it. I turned.

Shaeffer was standing with his feet planted wide apart. He could not have seen my action with the gun, not at that distance. The light was not good enough for that.

He said, "Get off the Garcia case, or I'll have your ass."

"For what?"

"Accomplice after the fact for helping Colquist get away."

I said, "I've been doing some thinking, Shaeffer, trying to put some things together."

"What things?"

"About you. About why you want me off this case so badly. You keep saying it's Harold Talent, but I think it's you."

"You're buying yourself a ton of trouble."

"I've already had trouble. Two guys jumped me today in Elinor Garcia's apartment. They'd been tipped off I'd be going there to turn up a lot of dirt on her."

He peered through the gloom at me. "You look okay to me."

"They had in mind rearranging my parts, but it didn't work out that way."

"Too bad," he said. "Got nothing to do with me."

"Know anybody named Max?"

"Maybe. What are you saying?"

"You wanted me scared off the Garcia thing, but you didn't want anybody to know it was you. So you tipped one of Alvera's boys to alert Elinor Garcia's cousins. One of the cousins fingered Max."

"Not a smart thing to do."

"He's safe. Anything happens to him, I step up to say you're the only one who knew. Not airtight, but you've got enough troubles without that. People might start scraping away your veneer and find a rotten cop underneath."

His hand started for his belt. I showed him the pointed bulge in my jacket pocket and said, "Don't." His hand relaxed back to his side. My eyes stared straight into his but they also watched his hands.

He said, "You'll go away a long time for this."

"Not for self-defense," I told him. "Crooked cop lures me down here at night. Plans to get rid of me because I know he's taking payoffs from underworld figures. But then there really isn't going to be any shooting, is there?"

He almost smiled. "That's right. No shooting. Why should I get upset over a story like that?"

"You shouldn't, unless I tagged you," I said. "But I think I did tag you. I think you're on Diaz's payroll. Who knows it?"

He shook his head. "Nuts."

"All right," I said. "I have enough to make some people curious. Who knows what a real investigation might turn up, including your connection with Manny Diaz?" I gave him a moment to think it over. "You shouldn't have reminded me of the old days, Shaeffer. I remembered you, you and your Corvette and all the girls. Girls are an expensive hobby, too expensive for a patrol officer."

74

He said, "We've got each other by the balls."

"It looks that way."

"I'm clean now, Broder. It wasn't easy to get clear of the Diaz bunch, but I did."

"Suppose I don't believe it."

"Makes no difference. You don't know anything."

"I know a name, Max: works for Alvera."

He took his time answering. Finally, he said, "Yeah. Max is one of Tommy's top boys. You stand about as much chance getting him to talk as getting Tommy to talk."

"So maybe you don't go to jail this year, but you'll land back in the slime. Alvera can use this over you, if I put on the pressure. As a price for their silence, they might want you back." I paused. "You made a bad mistake. You sent a couple of amateurs when you sent those Garcia cousins to work me over. When you start something like that, you better be sure you send enough muscle to finish the job."

"Shit. I figured the Garcias would get you off the case. I didn't figure to dig my own hole deeper."

"Maybe you should have sent Max himself."

"Yeah. Probably." He took a deep breath. He looked almost regretful. "What'll it be now?"

"I have to keep going. You get out of the way."

He shook his head. "It's my ass if you do."

"Who's putting on the heat? It can't be Diaz or Alvera. They'd know what to do about me."

He swore. "You're going to lose me my badge, Broder. After fifteen damn years, you're going to get me thrown off the goddam police force. And for what? For shit, that's what. Colquist killed that girl."

"Who's putting the heat on you?" I insisted.

"Who do you think? Whose wife are you trying to get into?"

I stood there for what seemed like a century while the implications of this statement filtered through a million connections in my brain. "Harold Talent?" I said at last. I could hear the note of disbelief in my own voice. "How would he know about your taking payoffs?"

"I don't know. He didn't say. I've thought about it plenty, too. But he knows, all right. He knows chapter and verse, the sonofabitch. The first time he came to me—that was Saturday—he wanted my sympathy and my cooperation. He suggested he would be an excellent possibility if I ever needed a co-signer on a loan. Today he got more serious. Today he brought up the money I took."

"It sounds like he knows somebody connected to Manny Diaz."

"The fuck it does. Who the hell cares? He really wants you out of his wife's life, Broder. Either that or it's my ass."

"It was his idea for you to threaten me with that accomplice-after-the-fact stuff?"

"Yeah. And if I go down, Broder, I'm taking you with me."

At that moment, in the uncertain light, his face held the look of a trapped animal. Desperation corroded his good looks, desperation that could drive him into unthinking action, possibly trying to draw on me even though my gun was already pointed at him.

I had to give him an out, or at least the appearance of an out. "Take it easy. Maybe we can figure something."

"Like what?"

"I don't know. I'm thinking. Suppose you had a couple of days. Could you work something out to get yourself off his hook?"

He rubbed his mouth with his hand. "I don't know. Shit, what the hell could I do?"

"Nice to have the time to think about it, wouldn't it? Maybe you can find out where Talent got his information. You want two days or don't you?"

"Fuck, yes. You going to lay off for that long?"

"You can tell Talent whatever you want to tell him. I could stay away from him"—I paused—"if I had another direction to go in."

"You want me to give you a lead."

"That's right. I know in any investigation there are always loose ends you could follow up if you had time. That's what I want from you."

"There's nothing there," Shaeffer replied. "I'm telling you, there's nothing in that file to change anybody's mind. Lots of shit, stuff you could go all over Tampa asking questions about, but it would get you nowhere."

He looked sincere, but you have to develop that look to become a successful ladies' man.

I said, "What about a guy named Diggs, Raymond Diggs?"

"Nothing about him."

"Sure," I said. "That's why you kept the file Garcia had on him. Of all Garcia's files, you sequestered only the ones on Colquist and this guy Diggs. I can understand your taking Colquist's folder, but why Diggs's?"

"It had Colquist's name in it."

"I see. In what connection?"

"His name was just noted next to some businesses that apparently supply to the laundromat trade."

"Diggs is in the laundromat business?"

"That's right. Why?"

"One of the Garcia cousins mentioned she had taken an interest in somebody who operates some laundromats. Same guy?"

He shrugged. "Could be. Anyway, I was curious because of the file, so I looked up Diggs. He had never heard of Garcia, so he said."

"When you showed him the file, he gave you a new story."

"Yeah. He said Garcia just wanted to make trouble for him. According to him, she had come on to him. He turned her down because he already has a girlfriend."

"And that made Garcia angry."

"Supposedly. Except we didn't believe it," replied Shaeffer. "She looked better dead than Diggs does alive."

"And then what?"

"Diggs started yelling for his lawyer, accusing us of harassing a small businessman because some floozie—that's what he called her—was making trouble all around."

"You let him get away with that?"

Shaeffer shrugged. "Why not? When she got it, he was in a bar with a dozen people who knew him."

"I'd say Diggs knows more about Garcia than he's willing to talk about," I suggested. "What's his background?"

He said, "Ordinary stuff. Worked here and there before going into business for himself. The guy's in his fifties. So maybe he's been somewhere or done something he doesn't want to talk about. Can't blame him for that."

"I think I better have a talk with Diggs. Where can I find him?"

"He runs a chain of coin laundries. Sunshine Coin-O-Matics, he calls them. He's heavy-set, has pinkish skin with a few big freckles, and thinning sandy hair. Go see him. Go see anybody. Just stay the hell away from the Talents."

"What do you plan to tell Talent?"

"I lie, that's what. I tell him you promised to let it alone." He paused. "And you tell his wife to keep her mouth shut about what you two are up to. Listen, if I can get Talent off my back, why, hell, there's no reason we can't work together on this. Sound good to you?"

"Good enough," I replied.

"Okay, we have a deal."

"Sure," I said. Sure, we had a deal, at least we did until he could figure out a way to get Talent—or me—off his case.

Shaeffer breathed out a load of trapped air. "Okay. I'll try to work something out. I don't know what, yet."

"Right," I agreed. "Why don't you pull out of here first, just in front of me." I wasn't sure whether Shaeffer planned to work something out to get rid of his problem with Talent or to get rid of his problem with me. And I felt a whole lot safer with him in front rather than behind me.

"Sure," he said. He saw my caution and pretended not to

see the reason for it. He hauled the sincere expression back to his face. "Sorry about that earlier," he added. "You got me wrong."

"Yeah," I said, and he smiled sincerely and went to his car and got in it and drove away.

We had a deal all right, the kind where you keep checking your back to see if there's a knife in it.

7

THE NEXT MORNING I went looking for Raymond Diggs, the guy on whom Elinor Garcia maintained a file. It could have turned out to be an exercise in futility, but I didn't have so many leads I could afford to ignore anyone, even a guy with an airtight alibi. The cops may not have found Diggs of any help, but the cops thought only Norm Colquist could have killed Garcia. I operated from the reverse premise, that only someone *besides* Norm could have. Therefore, I wanted to talk to Diggs and find out what made him so special to Elinor Garcia before she died, and why he didn't want to talk about it.

I found the fourth and last of the Sunshine Coin-O-Matics in a one-story block of storefronts on Dale Mabry. Diggs's business seemed to run itself. Apart from a black woman folding clothes for an absentee customer in the place on Gandy Boulevard, which was the second of his laundromats that I visited that morning, I found neither Diggs nor anyone else who worked for him. And the black woman said she saw him only on paydays.

I left the car on a side street and walked around the corner and went inside to an overheated, fluorescent world of laboring or spinning washers and tumbling dryers. Halfway along the center aisle that ran the length of the store between the machines, a man stood before a washer emptying its coin box into a blue cloth bag. He didn't match the description I had of Diggs, but if he were empowered to handle the quarters he must be part of Diggs's management team. I headed toward him.

I said, "I'm looking for Raymond Diggs."

He turned small black suspicious eyes in my direction. "He ain't here."

"Where can I find him?"

"He didn't say." The bag in his hand had a metal zipper across its top. He zipped it closed. "Who wants to know?"

I handed him my card.

He squinted at the card, held it at arm's length for a better look, and gave it back. "What's it about?"

"Elinor Garcia."

The man shrugged. "Don't know her."

One of his customers stood nearby with a plastic basket of laundry at her feet. We were blocking her access to the machine she wanted. The man slammed the coin box back into it and said to her, "It's all yours," and moved on to the next.

I followed him, with a ten tucked in my palm. "I'd like a word with Diggs," I said. "It's worth this." I showed him what I had in my hand.

He blinked and wiped his right hand on his blue denim pants. For an instant he seemed about to extend his hand for the ten. Then he looked at me, and a shadow flitted across his face, the look of a dull man whose dormant brain had just reminded him of something. He drew back and turned away from my glance.

"It has a brother," I said, coaxing.

He said, "I'm not Ray's keeper." His voice sounded sullen. "I just work here. Beat it." He pulled his coin-box key from the slot of the washer without unlocking the coin box. He started toward a door in the rear of the laundromat, next to a pay phone on the wall.

I went with him, through the door, into a tiny room lined with painted wood shelves. Cartons of laundry detergents and supplies, hand tools, and machine parts lay on the shelves.

"This is a private room," he said.

I shut the door. "It sure as hell is," I said, advancing toward him. His eyes looked suddenly scared. "Now," I went on. "Want to try that again? The part about not knowing anything about your boss?"

He dropped the bag of coins on the floor and retreated against the far shelves. "I just work here, mister," he whined. "I don't know nothing about Diggs."

"This is a cash business," I pointed out. "If Diggs trusts you enough to collect the money, he must trust you enough to let you know where he lives."

He swallowed heavily and licked his lips. "He lives in a hotel," he said. "The Imperial Palm. It's in Hyde Park."

"That's where you take the money?"

He shook his head. "I don't know. Ray said for me to call him when I got finished. Honest to God, mister, all I do is keep the place clean. This is the first time Ray ever asked me to empty the coin boxes. That's all I know."

He looked scared enough to be telling the truth. "Okay." I started out of the room, went back, and tucked the ten into his shirt pocket. "Maybe I'll surprise Ray," I said. "If you don't tell about this little talk, I won't either."

I walked briskly along the street to the entrance of one of the other shops in the row. The door was set back five or six feet from the sidewalk between the display windows. I could look out through the front display window and see a portion of the sidewalk in front of the laundromat. I had to wait only a few seconds before the man came out of the laundromat, stood on the sidewalk in the sunshine, and squinted up and down the street. Satisfied that I was out of sight, he hurried back into the laundromat.

When I walked past its entrance once more, he was in the rear of the place, engaged in an animated conversation on the pay phone. Somehow I didn't think Ray Diggs would be surprised to see me when I finally caught up to him.

The desk clerk who came to the counter at the Imperial Palm said, "Mr. Diggs isn't in. Key's in the box." He seemed to be in a hurry to get back to the magazine spread out on the little desk in the back corner.

"I'd have an extra key," I said, "if I lived in a hotel and wanted some privacy." I walked to the end of the counter that separated us and pointed to the house phone. "Mind if I try him myself?"

The clerk shrugged. "Four forty-five," he said and turned away, losing interest in me.

I let the phone ring ten times, with no result. "I'll wait," I said to the clerk. He ignored me.

I retreated to a worn and uncomfortable chair in a corner of the lobby. From there I could look across the lobby at the other worn and possibly equally uncomfortable furniture. The carpet, too, had seen better days, and the terrazzo floor, where not covered by the carpet, showed age cracks. But the place seemed clean and quiet, and maybe it would be a place I'd want if I wanted to live in a hotel, and if I could stomach the outside, five stories of pastel green stucco incongruously put down on a quiet street in Hyde Park.

From where I sat I had a view of the outside entrance into the lobby. Diggs could have gone out to eat. I decided to give him an hour.

After half that time I tried his room on the phone again and again got nothing. At the end of the full hour I tried the phone once more, with the same result. I went back to the clerk.

I said, "A man who lives alone in a hotel ought not to drink by himself. He'd have some place to go to do his drinking. Where does Diggs go?"

The clerk shrugged. "A place on Kennedy near West Shore." He gave me the name. "When he's expecting somebody he sometimes leaves word for them to go there and meet him." His eyes had a mixture of caution and curiosity in them. "He expecting you?"

"I thought he was," I replied. "Maybe he just forgot." I smiled at him, a little ruefully, as though the mistake had been mine. "I'll come back later," I added. I crossed the worn carpet and the terrazzo floor of the lobby toward the street and went out into the heat of the day.

The man who slouched against my car had black wavy hair and a black mustache and wore sunglasses. A small purple *M* was embroidered over the pocket of his lightweight white sport jacket. The jacket was buttoned. He probably wore his jacket for the same reason I wore mine: to conceal his gun. I guessed he'd have his tucked under his armpit. I didn't see it; I just knew it was there, from the look of him. As hot as it was, I couldn't think of any other good reason to wear a jacket.

He saw me and straightened up and said, "Broder?"

"That's right. Let me guess. You're Max."

He jerked a thumb toward a big white Lincoln Town Car parked farther down the street. "Somebody wants to see you."

"Uh-huh. Does somebody have a name?"

"Maybe. Move it, Jack. He doesn't like waiting."

I shrugged. "After you, *chico*."

His lips tightened, the only outward sign of his displeasure. He was young, not above twenty-five, probably, but disciplined. He turned and walked. I followed.

The car's windows, black with solar tinting, were all closed. The engine was running. Max opened the rear door and motioned me in. I could feel the cool air from the interior. I could see only a portion of the legs and butt of the man sitting on the other side of the rear seat.

"Thanks," I said and opened the front door and backed in, leaving the door open and keeping my feet on the sidewalk. I twisted to face the man in the rear.

The man slid to the right side of the car and pulled the rear door closed himself. He was a big man, but some of his bigness was turning to fat. He had a broad face with dark shadows. A white scar angled down from the corner of his mouth to his chin. His eyes focused on you, but you had to wonder what was going on behind them. They had an empty look.

"Hello, Broder," he said to me. To his driver he said, "Alone." That was all he needed to say.

The driver of the car slid out of his side of the car and joined Max in the narrow strip of shade under the palm trees. They both watched, not hearing the conversation between their boss and me, just watching.

"Hello, Tommy. It's been a while."

"Yeah. Three, four years, no? I bought you a drink. That was Manny's idea, not mine."

"I rather supposed it was. Manny's always been nice to people he couldn't buy off or scare off. How's he doing?"

"Not good. They got him hooked up to a lot of tubes and stuff. He's an old man. Had a long life. They oughta just let him go out peacefully."

"You figure to take over?"

He grunted. "Why not?"

"What about Al Connor?"

"I got the muscle."

"He's got the brains. Besides, his mother is Manny's niece."

The scar along Tommy Alvera's chin stood out as his cheeks hardened. "I never did like you much, Broder. Even when you were a smartass cop. Should have done something about it then. It's not too late. Remember that."

I didn't need the reminder that Tommy Alvera had come a long way since the night we first met in a singles bar. He was trying to persuade a girl to come with him. She tired of him and, not knowing who he was, called him a jerk to his face, in front of other people. He slapped her around, hard, and was in the process of dragging her out when I arrived. I put him down, took his gun, and cuffed him. He never forgot it.

"What did you want to see me about?" I asked.

He looked out his solar-tinted window toward Diggs's hotel. "I hear you're asking around about a friend of mine."

"Who might that be, Tommy?"

He turned his eyes back to me. "Ray Diggs. What's it about, Broder?"

I allowed my surprise to show. "Diggs? Well, well, that does make Mr. Diggs interesting."

The scar stood out once more. "I asked you a question, Broder. What's it about?"

"It's about murder. That's what makes it so interesting, seeing that murder is your line of work, Tommy. Want to know more?"

He said he did so I continued. "A girl named Elinor Garcia wound up with five bullets in her. She hustled business deals, more or less legitimate stuff, I gather. She and Diggs were acquainted. She was running a little file on his business. He may not have liked it, though he told the cops he didn't know anything about it."

"What was in the file?"

"Nothing against Diggs, apparently. Nothing that would give him any reason to shoot her." I paused, briefly. "Did you know her?"

Alvera said, "No. Heard about it, though."

"She wouldn't have somehow gotten in your way, would she?"

Alvera laughed without warmth, without humor. "You figuring to hang it on me?"

"If you had it done, there wouldn't be any way to hang it on you." I paused to look across the sidewalk at his two gunnies. "Besides," I went on, looking back to Alvera, "if she had been mixed up with the mob, I'd have heard about it by now."

"You have your troubles, Broder. Tough shit. Just leave Diggs out of it. Out of anything."

"What's he doing for you guys?"

86

Alvera hesitated, uncertainty in the working of his mouth, his eyes hidden. "Nothing," he said at last. "Ray used to tend bar at the old Shadows nightclub."

"Manny's old place?"

"That's right. Manny liked Ray. Gave him a couple of breaks. Ray's doing okay now. Strictly legit. Manny would hate to see Ray harassed, just because he's a friend."

I slid partway out of the car. "Then tell Diggs to stand till long enough for some talk with me. If he's on the outside of the Garcia killing, I'm finished with him. I'm not after you or your business or your friends. I'm not that stupid."

I gave Max and his friend one glance before turning back to Alvera. I patted the upholstery on the front seat. "Nice car, Tommy. If this doesn't get you a girl, nothing will." I slid the rest of the way out of the car.

"You're a sonofabitch, Broder," said the voice I left behind.

I waved to the two gunnies and walked away, feeling an itch between my shoulder blades. I was right. Tommy Alvera had not forgotten the night we met. Maybe it was stupid to bait him like that, but the urge had come over me before I had the good sense to think about it.

On the other hand, I told myself, as I reached my own car and sat there watching the big Lincoln drive away, if you think about a guy like Tommy Alvera too long, it makes you too cautious. To Tommy, caution could look like fear, and the scent of fear in Alvera's nostrils always brought out the bully in him. Maybe the urge I had felt was an act of instinctive self-defense, letting Tommy know I wasn't afraid of him. Like a dog's bark, I told myself a little uneasily, knowing that against Alvera's guns the shortfall between my bark and my bite could be fatal. To me.

On my way to Ray Diggs's favorite watering hole, I stopped at the same McDonald's on Kennedy Boulevard where I had met Talent. This time I went in, as a sort of recompense for my free use of the parking lot the night before. I ate a large cheeseburger and fries and a milk shake and used their pay phone to call my answering service. Amy was on duty and said Margaret Talent had called. She needed to see me. Right away. At her tennis club. Directions provided. I decided anything Diggs's bartender could tell me would have to wait. I was a dozen blocks or so from Tampa Bay and where Margaret played her tennis. I put on my sunglasses and went out into the early afternoon brightness and turned the Chevy toward the water.

I parked the car in the parking lot in the shade of a large old live oak festooned with Spanish moss. I went in and left my name and returned to the car and waited. Fifteen minutes later, Margaret marched across the pavement with determined purpose in her stride. She'd always looked good in her tennis whites, and she still did, even though battling the world.

She slid into the car beside me, her face drawn and weary. "They found Norman," she said.

"I know. I'm sorry, Margaret."

"We knew it would be like that, didn't we?"

"Yes." I paused. "What did you want to see me about?"

She stared at me for a long moment. "Have you dropped the case?" she asked softly, her voice sounding almost defeated.

"Talent tell you that?"

"Yes," she said. "This morning. Just so there would be no doubt, he had the police officer also tell me. The evidence against Norman is overwhelming, and you decided to drop the case because it was hopeless."

"That's the story you were supposed to hear."

She shook her head in bafflement. "I don't understand."

"Let's walk," I suggested.

A narrow driveway surrounded the complex of tennis courts, squash courts, pool, clubhouse, and parking area.

Part of the driveway bordered a wide canal. We walked along the canal. Across from us, long low private homes with screened pool enclosures and private docks lined the canal's opposite side.

I said, "I talked to Shaeffer last night. He cooked up that story then. He's covering his own ass. That's all it comes to. I'm still on the case."

"Last night?" she said. "Then why didn't you call me? Why did you let me go through all that, not knowing?"

"Because you would not have reacted naturally if you had known. Either you would have sat there impassively, knowing you were hearing a lie, or you would have tried to put on an act. Your husband would have seen through either of those things. Instead, he got exactly what he expected—the reaction of a woman with the ground cut out from under her—and now you're doing exactly what he would expect you to do—come to me to find out what's going on."

She shook her head. "I had to know. Especially after last night, after the news about Norman. They say his body was so . . . so bad that . . ."

"Yes. I know."

"And then Harold this morning, and the detective. You can't know what it was like. I don't know how much more I can take."

I stopped in front of her and faced her. "It's bad, and it may get worse, and you're going to have to take whatever comes along."

"Because I started it. Is that what you mean?"

"No. I mean this: we're in it together because neither one of us wanted to leave it alone when Norm left. Maybe we should have, but we didn't, and maybe it's too late now. Maybe I've opened too many doors, doors that weren't supposed to be opened, doors that can't be closed again."

"What is it, Paul? What's going on?"

I told her about Ray Diggs. I also told her about Tommy Alvera. "I'm not telling you this to scare you. You just ought

89

to know that the bets go up when Tommy Alvera sits in the game."

"A gangster? Why?"

"Not just any gangster, Margaret. Tommy Alvera is the chief enforcer for Manny Diaz."

"What does he have to do with any of us?" She paused to reflect on her question. "Was Norman in debt to those people?"

We resumed our stroll along the canal before I answered her. "He told me his trouble was not with the Diaz bunch, and he sounded as though he meant it. No, Alvera's interest is in Diggs, not Garcia or Norm. If it bothered him that I was investigating either of those deaths, he'd have said so. He wouldn't have bothered making up a story about Diggs."

"Then what is it?"

"There's something more going on here," I went on. "Something other than gambling debts. I don't know what it is. I just feel it, like a far shadow on a wall at night, a shadow that shouldn't be there."

"You sound as though you know him, this Alvera."

"I do."

She shuddered, seized by a sudden chill, though she walked under the hot afternoon sun along the concrete wall of the canal. She stopped and looked up at me. "You live surrounded by violence, Paul Broder. You always have. That's what made me leave, nothing else. Did you know?"

"I knew. You shouldn't have come back for my help."

"I told you why I did. I trust you, and my brother didn't kill that girl. Did he?"

"No. Someone else did, and that someone wants Norm to take the fall."

"We assumed that from the beginning," she reminded me.

"No assumption now, Margaret. I know. Our someone made a mistake by planting the gun that killed Garcia on the body, hoping the cops would think Norm had it with him." I stopped where the driveway curved away from the canal.

"Norm didn't have a gun when he came to see me that night. He asked if I would give him one. I didn't."

You could see the pieces falling into place behind her eyes. She said, "So the gun that killed Elinor Garcia was left with Norm's body to make him look guilty."

"Yes," I agreed. "And, knowing that, we know Norm was innocent."

"You have to go to the police with that," she said. You could see the triumph in her eyes. "It's what we've been looking for, enough evidence to make the police reopen their investigation."

"No. It's only supposition and my word. Not enough. Shaeffer's in too much trouble. He'll stonewall, maybe worse. He can't afford to reopen the case."

"It's his job," she said.

"Your husband could ruin him, and your husband doesn't want me investigating the Garcia thing."

"I can't believe that. Why?"

"Shaeffer says it's because of jealousy. You and I spending too much time together gives your husband heartburn." She looked at me with startled eyes, and I added, quickly, "I think there's more to it." I paused, thinking back. "Talent told me he had met Elinor Garcia only once, at your home. I assumed at the time it was the truth. I'm not sure now. Do you know of any reason to doubt him?"

"You're not suggesting that Harold had anything to do with her death?"

"No. Norm told me that Talent was in Naples about the time Garcia was killed. That's a two- or three-hour drive. No way he could have been in both places at the same time."

She didn't ask how Norm knew his brother-in-law was in Naples. That spared me telling her how her husband turned down her brother's pleas for help. She didn't need that. She had something else to decide.

"Look, Margaret. I don't know what's in front of us if I go on. I can't predict anything."

91

"And if you stop?" she asked and looked at me steadily. "What about those doors you've already opened?"

"I don't know that either. If it were just me, I'd go ahead."

"Because that's the only direction you know," she said. "I'm not like that. That's why you're offering to give it up. Because it will get worse, and I'm afraid."

"You have more at stake than I do."

"Yes, I do, don't I? But we can't stop now, not when we *know* Norman didn't kill that girl."

We had retraced our steps to my car. She looked up at me and said, "Ten years ago I walked out on you because I was scared, scared I'd lose you to a bullet in a dark alley. I couldn't face that because I depended on you too much. I had to get away from you, break that dependence on you. Funny, isn't it? Now you're all I have left to depend on."

Then I found out why she had not asked me about how Norm knew Talent was in Naples. She already suspected something.

She said, "I told Harold today it was inconceivable for Norman to leave town with gangsters after him without asking us for the money to cover his debts. Harold assured me he had not heard from him. Did he lie?"

"Yes." I told her about Norm's phone calls to Naples.

She shook her head and stared at a chameleon skittering across the edge of the blacktop. "I suppose I knew it all along and didn't want to believe it. And now my brother is dead." She looked up and heaved a deep sigh. "I've come back to you, then, when I needed help. After all these years, you could tell me to go to hell, pay me back for walking out on you."

I took her by the shoulders and held her and looked in her eyes. "Stop it, Margaret. I got over that a long time ago, and you should too. We live different lives. I've made mine what it is, and you've made yours the way you wanted it. So you're having a hard time now, sure, but that will pass and everything will be back to where it was. It's no good talking about who might pay who back. That was never us, and you know it." I took a deep breath and released her. "Go back to your husband and tell him you've fired me. For incompetency or whatever."

She stepped back, her eyes bright and hard on mine. "I'll tell him," she said. "About the other, I don't know."

"What other?"

"Going back to him," she said and shrugged. "I'll go to the house we both live in. That's where my children are. That's not the same as going back to him. That may happen, or it may not. You could be right. Maybe it will all pass. I'll just have to see, won't I?"

I called the bar where Diggs did his drinking and got a husky-voiced waitress on the telephone. No, she told me, she hadn't seen Ray Diggs. She called to somebody whose name I failed to hear, and a man's voice in the background said, "Ain't seen him. Tell him to try around four or so this afternoon."

I thanked the waitress and hung up without giving my name. I had the distinct impression that Ray Diggs was avoiding people, especially anyone he didn't know, like me. He had pulled out of the Imperial Palm in a hurry when he heard I was looking for him. That made me even more curious about him than Shaeffer had made me.

When Tommy Alvera got into the act, I became downright fascinated. Alvera was the heavy artillery. Just because he didn't like me personally was no reason for him to want a hand dealt in any game I was playing. He and I had managed to coexist in Tampa for quite a few years. No, it wasn't me that made Alvera want to keep me away from Diggs, and it wasn't that yarn he'd tried to spin about Diggs being an old pal of Manny Diaz.

It was Diggs. But what was it about Ray Diggs that made him so important? I decided I had better find out. It was several hours yet before it was time to call the husky-voiced waitress again. Between calls I could use the time to look for Ray Diggs in my own way.

The last thing that I could expect him to do was to hang around that Kennedy Boulevard saloon with one foot on the rail and one elbow on the bar, waiting for the cavalry to show up.

8

EAST TAMPA WAS out of my way, but it was where I knew I could find what I needed, which was an evil-looking switchblade knife. The man I bought it from gave me a yellow-toothed grin and said, "Who the fuck you gon' cut, man?" Not, of course, that it made any difference to him. He handed it to me wrapped in toilet paper, took his money, and slid out of the car.

I took the Crosstown Expressway back through the city and exited on Gandy Boulevard. I looked for a liquor store. When I found one, I pulled in and bought a half pint of cheap gin. The gin went with me, unopened, to my car. Gin isn't my favorite alcoholic beverage, but it leaves a pronounced drinking odor on the breath. That odor was what I wanted.

I also wanted Ray Diggs, but going back to his hotel wasn't the smartest thing I could do. Tommy Alvera might have put a man in the lobby, or he might have told the desk clerk to let him know if I came around again. You can't let a hood like Alvera scare you out of doing your job or you won't be in business long, but he had the muscle to block me if I went at him head on.

The idea was to get to Diggs before Alvera knew about it. That meant I had to avoid the obvious places and take the long way around. The first thing to do was call the hotel and see if Diggs had returned.

I told the desk clerk, "Hi. This is Ted at Carson Cleaning Supply. Ring Ray in four forty-five, please."

Diggs had not returned. Either that or he was holed up in his room, not answering the phone. I would have liked to know for sure, but there was no way to get to his room without the desk clerk's okay. The hour spent in the hotel lobby waiting for Diggs and analyzing all the ways into the building showed me that. Once the shift changed at the desk, another possibility would open up, but for now the desk clerk at the Imperial Palm was one of the people I needed to stay away from.

The other person to avoid was the guy collecting coins at the laundromats. As soon as he thought I was out of sight, he got on the phone to somebody. An hour and a half later, Tommy Alvera showed up. There had to be another way. I hoped the gin and the knife would get me started.

I parked in a Hardee's parking lot and used their men's room to drink some of the gin and gargle and rinse my mouth with most of the rest. What remained I used to soak paper towels rolled into two little balls. I put a gin-soaked paper ball in each cheek and walked two blocks to the Sunshine Coin-O-Matic. I was glad to get rid of the gin balls in a litter can.

I found the black woman reaching into an open washer and building a mound of wet clothing in a yellow plastic basket on the floor by her feet. She didn't look up until I stood next to her.

"Wanna see Diggs, missus," I said. I put out one hand and leaned on her washer.

She winced at the smell of the gin. "He ain't come back," she said. "Come back tomorrow. Or try one of the other places." She recognized me from earlier. I had supposed she would. "Been everywhere, missus, and I'm done playing."

She shook her head with disgust. "Git outa here and go home and sober up and leave honest people to their work." She bent back to her labor.

I counted off a silent ten seconds before speaking again. I said, "He's messing with my woman, missus."

She went on unloading the wet load from the washer, ignoring me. I took the knife from my pocket and snapped the blade out to its business position. Her back stiffened like a poker. She had heard that sound before.

She turned slowly, backing away, eyeing the blade. "Whatever you want, white man, I ain't got it."

"If I find Ray Diggs, missus, I'm fixing to cut him." I breathed heavily in her direction. "He won't need no woman if I find him." I pushed the blade into the handle and pocketed the knife.

She looked relieved. "That's bad business, mister."

I nodded my head solemnly. "Yeah," I said. "I know. But how'm I gonna keep him away from my woman, if I don't? I hear tell he's already got a woman, and I'd tell her, but I don't know her. Maybe she could put a leash on him."

"Go home and sleep it off, mister." Her face began to look more sympathetic.

"You know his woman, missus?" I pleaded. "I don't want to cut nobody, but I will if I have to."

The black woman hesitated, but only for a moment. "He's come in a couple of times with a blond woman. He calls her Mary Alice, and she talks a lot. That's all I know."

I nodded and told her I was tired and walked stiffly out of the place, like a drunk trying his best not to stagger.

The bartender at the place on Kennedy Boulevard moved behind the bar in my direction. The place was nearly empty. Only one other man stood at the bar. One couple sat at a table along the wall opposite the bar.

The place was dark, mostly. The only light came from several fake-Tiffany-shaded ceiling lamps spaced well apart. On the walls hung dusty old swords and shields and pewter beer mugs. The chairs and tables were dark wood, and the chairs had arms and seats covered in black plastic like the seats of the stools at the bar.

The bartender had been talking to a waitress when I arrived. I supposed it was the husky-voiced woman who had answered the telephone. She moved off toward the kitchen when he headed for me and asked what I'd have.

"Draft," I told him, and he brought it, and I told him that it was ten degrees cooler in Tampa than it had been in Miami, and he asked me if I lived in Miami.

I put my hand over the bar and said, "Bill Downs." It was the name on one of the business cards I carried in my pocket.

In answer to the bartender's question about whether I lived in Miami, I said Miami Springs, and he said he used to work at a lounge near the airport, and we talked about places we both knew.

I looked at my watch several times during our talk.

"Supposed to meet an old friend and her guy here," I said, shaking my head. "I don't get up here much. You wouldn't happen to know a blond girl named Mary Alice, would you?" What I needed was Mary Alice's last name and her address or phone number or both. But the last name came first. After that there was always the phone book.

He beamed at me but didn't give me what I wanted. "Mary Alice? Ray Diggs's girl. Sure, they're regulars. Little early for them, though."

"Yeah," I agreed. "I'd better give her a call." I took my well-used notebook out of my jacket pocket and pushed a dollar bill toward him. He gave me change and sent me in the direction of a sign that said KNIGHTS AND LADIES. I used the pay phone in the hall next to the toilets, tapping out Norm Colquist's number. It rang and rang. I hung up and went back to the bar. "No answer?" asked the bartender.

I shook my head. "I sure as hell don't want to miss her, but I have to head back soon. The people I work for get antsy when I'm gone too long." I got out the worn notebook again and thumbed through it. "All I've got is her number, no address," I said and looked hopeful. "You wouldn't know where she lives, would you?"

"Sorry," he said. "Out in Temple Terrace, I think, but then a lot of people live out there. Is she in the phone book?"

I shook my head. "No." Still no last name.

"Hey," said the bartender. "Where's my head today? She works in a beauty parlor only three or four blocks from here. Place called the Hair and Now."

I gathered up my change, except for two ones, and said, "Best I go on over there and see her for a minute or so and head back to Miami."

"Yeah," he agreed, keeping his eyes from looking at the two ones. "Get up this way again, man, stop in."

"I'll do that," I said, and left.

I parked at the side of the Hair and Now beauty salon, pointing the car in toward the blank cinder-block wall facing the tiny blacktopped parking lot. I sat there for a moment considering what I wanted from Mary Alice and what I'd settle for. What I wanted was for her to tell me where Ray Diggs was and then keep quiet about it until I had my mitts on him. What I would settle for was for her to get a message to him that, if he hadn't killed Elinor Garcia, I'd be no trouble to him, and, if he had killed her, hiding from me wasn't going to solve his problem.

In the event, I got neither what I wanted nor what I'd settle for nor anything in between. I walked into the air conditioning and saw just the top of a blond head. The rest of the woman was seated behind a high counter which was faced in oak paneling and topped with Formica. Beyond, through the opening in the partition behind the counter, two women were being worked on. All around me hung photos of what those two hoped they'd look like when the work was done.

I approached the counter and asked for Mary Alice, figuring the girl seated behind the counter working on an appointment book could not have been Mary Alice. The blonde I saw was in her early twenties, too young for Ray Diggs, assuming he had any sense, that is. I was right. She wasn't Mary Alice. Mary Alice had the afternoon off.

"Working on her tan," said the blonde. She showed me a nice smile.

"Just my luck," I said and smiled back. "Haven't seen her for a hundred years, and I have to head back to Miami in an hour or so."

"She'll be sorry she missed you. She always says that a person can't have too many friends."

She didn't volunteer Mary Alice's address, so an awkward moment of silence passed between us.

I was about to ask her for the address when my thinker warned me against such a direct approach. The blonde wasn't about to hand out Mary Alice's address to a strange man who walked in claiming to be an old friend. She needed more convincing.

Something that the woman in the laundromat told me about Mary Alice came to my rescue, something to the effect that Mary Alice liked to talk. I chased the recollection around in my mind for a half second until it came to me how I could use it.

"Use your phone?" I asked the girl in front of me. "If she's home, she can give me directions how to get out to her place."

"Sure," she said. She handed her phone up to me, and I put it on the counter. She bent her head and poised her pencil over the appointment book spread out in front of her. That was to give the illusion of privacy.

I punched out the number of my cable TV service department, always a useful number to know when you want a busy signal. I held the receiver away from my face and let the blonde have the benefit of hearing a couple of busy beeps.

I put the receiver down and handed the phone back to her. "I could be halfway to Miami by the time she gets off the phone," I said. "You know Mary Alice."

She giggled and agreed that she knew Mary Alice. I took one of the Bill Downs cards from my wallet and said, "Tell her I'm sorry I missed her. I probably have her address at

100

home, but all I have with me is her phone number."

She was convinced. "I can give you her address," she said, "if you think you can find your way out there, Mr. Downs." She smiled again, and said, "Bill." She wrote out the address on a note pad and handed me the sheet.

I took it and told her I'd give it a try and flirted with her just enough so that she wouldn't have second thoughts and call Mary Alice before I got there.

She came to the door wearing a black bikini. She was about forty and had a fold of skin around her ribs and belly between the top and the bottom of the bathing suit. She was shiny all over and smelled of coconut oil. She held the door open about a foot and said, "Yes?"

"It's about Ray," I said. "Can we talk inside?"

A scared look came to her eyes, and she backed into the apartment. "What's wrong? What is it?"

Her apartment was on the ground floor. The front entrance was partially enclosed by a seven-foot-high wall to give callers a sense of privacy. Inside the wall were some plants rooted in the soil below a gravel mulch. It was like a little tropical garden. Nice. More than she could afford, probably, without a little help from her friend.

There were, I guessed, twenty or so apartments in the place, all on two floors with an outside balcony running the length of the building. It lay on a dead-end street, three blocks from the only intersection where Mary Alice would have a choice of directions to turn. Just past the intersection was an Exxon station with a pay phone. I had used that telephone before I returned to Mary Alice's parking lot, parked my car, and knocked at her front door.

I went in and shut the door behind me and said, "So far as I know, he's okay." That was to bring her back down from the near panic I had seen in her eyes. She could worry as much as she felt the need to. That was okay with me, but I didn't want her hysterical. I added, "For the time being, that

101

is."

"Who are you?" she demanded, retreating two more steps.

"The name is Broder, and I'm looking for your boyfriend. And if I don't find him soon, I'm going to get nasty as hell."

Her eyes looked scared. She said, "I don't know anything about his business or where he's at."

He would have told her to say that.

"Don't be a fool, sweetheart. I'm not out to hurt Diggs. I'll leave that to his friends, guys like Tommy Alvera."

Color drained from her face. The name Alvera meant something to her. Diggs must have told her about Alvera's reputation for the mere mention of the name to have drawn such a reaction.

I went on. "Alvera told me to stay away from Diggs," I said. "In my book that means Diggs knows something Alvera doesn't want him to tell me. I'm glad I'm not in Diggs's shoes. Alvera has ways of keeping people from talking, if he thinks there's a chance they might."

She seemed to have a hard time breathing. "No, Ray don't know nothing," she said, her voice strained. It was a north Florida voice, more southern than you usually hear around Tampa. "Honest to Jesus."

"He knows more about the Garcia murder than he's told."

She shook her head violently. "No. You're lying. Ray said you wanted to make it look like someone else had killed her . . ."—she stopped in mid-sentence and swallowed heavily— "because you used to be married to the real killer's sister."

"Diggs said that, did he? Now how do you suppose he knows so much about me?" I didn't expect an answer, and I didn't get one. I took out one of my cards and shoved it into her hand. "Tell your boyfriend I want to talk to him. Tell him I know about Elinor Garcia running a file on him. You might also ask him if Alvera knows about that."

I turned and left her and walked out to the parking lot, where I had left my car, out there in the open, parked between the yellow lines on the blacktop that marked the guest parking spaces.

The residents parked under a flat steel-roofed carport, where their cars stood protected from the hot sun. I figured the car belonging to Ray Diggs's girlfriend would be parked in one of the reserved spaces close to her front door. It was, and it wasn't difficult to tell which one it was. It was a blue Chevette.

I felt fairly confident she would carry the message to Diggs about me wanting to see him. Whether or not Diggs would voluntarily come forward was another matter. He was worried about something he didn't want me to know about or something he didn't want someone else to worry about my finding out. Whatever it was, it had been enough to chase him out of his comfortable and familiar surroundings at the Imperial Palm.

He might decide to talk to me, or he might not. I couldn't count on it or wait forever for him to make up his mind. If he wouldn't come to me, I had to wait for him to see Mary Alice, or I had to go to him. That was why I had made the telephone call from the Exxon station before knocking on Ray Diggs's girlfriend's door.

I went to my car and opened the door and felt the solar-heated interior air roll over me, released by the opening of the door. I stood there for a moment, letting the inside of the car breathe a little. As I stood there, I glanced toward Mary Alice's apartment and saw the drapery move. Checking, I supposed, to be sure I had left before she called Diggs for instructions.

I was figuring that she'd want to see him, that she'd be too upset at my visit to be satisfied with just a telephone call. She'd want his assurance, she'd have to meet him. It wasn't the sort of thing she could get over the phone.

Or so I supposed. It was only a thought, possibly only a wishful thought, but it was worth setting up for, just in case. I'd soon see.

103

I drove the car out of the parking lot toward the Exxon station. I expected that the woman I had called from there would soon be arriving. I wasn't disappointed. She arrived, driving a shabby brown Ford Escort, after I had waited about ten or fifteen minutes. She pulled in beside my car. I got out and walked to hers and got in.

Yvonne was her name, and she had helped me with other little tasks in the past. She was a part-timer who was good enough to have worked full-time for any agency if she had wanted to. But she didn't need a full-time paycheck, and she liked to watch four hours of soap operas every day, which is what she was doing when I called earlier.

I apologized, and she said, "That's the beauty of a VCR."

"I just left her," I said. "I figure she'll be calling Diggs about now. I'll go back and spot myself where I can see if Diggs shows up. If she goes out, I'll follow her. She has to come by here."

"She'd just come from the pool?" asked Yvonne. I said she had.

"She'll have to call him first and then shower off the coconut oil," observed Yvonne. "And do something about her hair. She'll also have to dress and put on some makeup and perfume. This is her boyfriend she's going to see, Broder, not her mother. I'll be right here. What kind of car?"

"A blue Chevette. You'll know you have the right car when you see the bumper sticker. It says *Beauticians do it with style*."

Diggs's girlfriend came out of her apartment forty minutes later and drove past me in her blue Chevette. I was parked in the parking lot of the apartment adjacent to hers, trying to look inconspicuous. I pulled onto the street behind her as she passed. I could see her glance into her rearview mirror.

She went in the only direction she could go in, toward the Exxon station. As she approached the traffic light she began slowing for it, although it still showed green. As she neared

104

the intersection, the light went yellow. She accelerated through the intersection just as the light turned red, leaving me stopped as the cross traffic began to move.

As she pulled away from me, I could see her hold up her right hand and wiggle her fingers at me in a triumphant good-bye-sucker gesture. She was happy, so happy she would never notice the woman in the nondescript brown Escort who pulled out of the Exxon station and into the traffic behind her.

Lori, at my answering service, had a message for me. The man wouldn't give his name. He told Lori he could tell me something about Norm Colquist. If I were interested, he said, I should meet him at the bar in the Floridan Hotel downtown. He'd be sitting alone at the corner table on the right between five and six o'clock.

I wasn't sure when I'd hear from my friend tailing Diggs's girlfriend so I headed for town, parked on Cass, and walked around the corner to the hotel entrance. The Floridan is an older place on the fringes of the downtown boom. As I went in the entrance off Florida Avenue, the bar was through a door to the left. The place was small and dark and crowded. The bar at the far end of the room was lined with men, and most of the tables were occupied. I saw only three women.

The man I looked for was right where he said he'd be, at the little round table in the corner. He was sipping a shot of whiskey and chasing it with beer when I arrived. I ordered him another round, nothing for myself. I didn't have much time. Diggs was the important one, not a fifty-ish barfly wearing a secondhand suit who wouldn't tell me his name.

But he had mine, and I wanted to know how and why.

"You used to be married to Norm Colquist's sister," he said. "Norm mentioned you lots. I remembered your name, and you're in the book. Yellow pages, too. I looked." He seemed pleased that he had tracked me down.

"You a friend of Norm's?" I asked.

"That's right," he said. "I knew Norm in GA."

"I heard he had a problem a couple of years ago."

"Yeah. Me, I didn't stick around very long. Christ, a man's gotta have a little fun out of life. Wasn't my idea anyway. My ex-wife insisted. Said if I didn't straighten out, she'd divorce me. Well, she did anyway, and I never been happier."

"About Norm," I reminded him.

"Let me tell it, will you? Look, about six months ago I'm busted, see? So I figure I'd try GA again, not having anything better to do. Anyway, Norm was still there, and I really think he was glad to see me back." He paused to sip some whiskey. "Didn't work any better the second time than it did the first, but Norm tried to help me. That's what he figured he was doing, anyhow. Then today I see this."

He shoved a folded Tampa newspaper toward me and pointed out the article he meant.

> The body of a man believed to be Norman Colquist, wanted for the murder of a Tampa woman, was discovered by officers from the Duval County Sheriff's Department last night. The discovery was made about two miles east of Baldwin, near Interstate 10.
>
> Colquist, believed heavily in debt to underworld gambling interests, had been shot three times in the back of the head. The body, according to sheriff's deputies on the scene, was . . ."

I had read enough. I slid the paper across the table and said, "So?"

"It's a lie," said the man, "a goddamned lie. I figured his family ought to know it was a lie, so I called his brother-in-law, Talent. You know him?"

"I know him. Go on."

"Secretary said he went up to Baldwin to identify the body. Secretary didn't know shit. She told me to call the cops."

"Instead, you called me."

"Yeah. I figured you could tell the cops yourself and set

things straight and keep me out of it. I need cops like I need another wife."

A man approached. He looked at me and asked, "Are you Paul Broder?"

"That's right."

"There's a call for you. Phone's in the lobby."

"Tell whoever it is to hold on," I said. "And thanks." I turned back to the man sitting across from me. "What things?"

"That shit about Norm stiffing the mob. Listen, Broder, Norm Colquist never laid a bet in the last two years. He didn't owe anybody a goddam dime, and that's a plain fact."

9

I THREADED MY way out through the crowd to the lobby and found the phone and picked up the receiver. I said, "This is Broder."

"The beautician went to a motel about five miles up Two seventy-five," said the woman on the other end. "It's called the Night's Rest. She parked in front and went up to room two fourteen. That's on an open balcony, second floor front. The man who came to the door was middle-aged and overweight, ruddy face, thinning hair. He's registered under the name of Draper."

"That's Diggs. Did he spot you?"

"I don't think so, but you can never be a hundred percent sure."

"I know. Thanks, Yvonne. Send me the bill." I hung up and returned to the bar and to the man who had told me that Norm had not gambled recently and owed no money to underworld gambling interests or to anyone else. I bought him two whiskeys, and when the second was gone he was as certain of his story as before. I couldn't shake him, and I couldn't change his mind, and I hadn't time to stay in the bar and argue with him.

I wanted to see Diggs before he got fidgety. Mary Alice might have put him in the mood for a little playtime. That would keep him awhile, but not forever. After a party he might take a more serious look at how good Mary Alice would be at shaking surveillance and he might not like the conclusion he'd come to. I had to get moving.

I put money on the table for the drinks and headed for my

car and a visit with Raymond Diggs.

I pulled off I-275 onto a side street and turned almost immediately into the parking lot of the motel to which Diggs's girlfriend had driven. I drove around the two-story building to a nearly empty parking lot in the rear.

Diggs's room, as Yvonne had told me, was on the second floor and faced to the front, with a view overlooking the entrance to the parking lot.

I went up an open stairway and walked along the balcony to 214. I heard no sound from inside the room. I tried the doorknob, gently. It did not turn. The door was locked. I knocked. The knock brought forth no response from within the room. I knocked again. All remained still.

I went back down the stairs and walked to the office and said to the woman behind the counter, "Draper in two fourteen. He doesn't answer. Can you check to see if everything is all right?"

She shook her head. "Draper checked out nearly a half hour ago. That room is vacant."

I walked back across the parking lot pavement to my car and slid in behind the wheel and sat watching lights flicker on around me. Night follows day quickly in Florida, allowing little time for the lingering twilight of more northern latitudes.

Had Diggs spotted the tail on his girlfriend? Maybe, though I doubted it. Yvonne was too good to let that happen. Diggs probably started from the premise that his girlfriend wasn't too smart. She'd have told him how easily she had dropped me; that alone might have made him suspicious. So he moved fast, like a man trying to stay alive, not a man trying to avoid a few questions.

I started the engine. All that was useless thinking. Diggs had disappeared again and either took his girlfriend with him or was not likely to tell her where he was going this time.

What was important was that I had to start all over again to find him, since he was the one person who could tell me about Elinor Garcia, about what made her so important to Norm Colquist that Norm felt compelled to leave town because of her, and to someone else who felt compelled to shoot her.

I drove downtown to the bright lights and called the answering service and told Lori where I'd be, which was at a restaurant that serves a three-egg omelet with cheese and ham and mushrooms. Diggs could have a change of heart, and I wanted him to be able to find me when or if he did.

I was working on my second bottle of beer and was halfway through the omelet when a man's voice spoke my name. I looked up and saw Harold Talent standing three feet away.

He said, "I want to talk to you, but I'll wait until you've finished, if you prefer."

"Sit down," I invited. "Neither of us would be happy waiting."

He sat opposite me and ordered a whiskey from the waiter and asked me if I wanted anything, and I said I was fine.

He said, "I brought Norm's body back from Baldwin today. There'll be a small service tomorrow at the crematorium for family and very close friends. No viewing, of course." Then came the hard part for him. "Naturally, you're welcome to attend. I mean, in view of—"

I cut him off. "Thanks, but no thanks."

Suspicion clouded his eyes. He may have thought I turned down his offer of a truce so I could make a more dramatic entrance.

I said, "People go to funerals because it's the last thing they can do for the corpse. It helps you make up for all the things you should have done before the death: squaring one's moral debts, so to speak. Well, I may owe Norm something, but it's a debt that can't be paid by going to his funeral."

Talent's eyes narrowed. "Margaret told me she had let you

110

go, that you were no longer working for her."

"That's right. Now I'm working for me, paying off what I owe Norm."

"What do you owe him, Broder?"

"Nothing tangible, probably. It's just a feeling that comes from the sort of person Norm was. When he was alive, he always worked the sympathy angle whenever he could. That was part of the way he was when he knew he had you hooked."

"Yes," replied Talent. He smiled without warmth. "If you let him do it, he would. It was easy to see with Margaret. She was his sister and two years older. He was quite good at making her feel a certain sibling responsibility."

I said nothing in response. A silence fell between us. He broke it, speaking as he looked down at his whiskey.

"I have a message for you," he said. "I understand you're looking for a man named Raymond Diggs."

"You get around. Shaeffer tell you that?"

He shook his head. "Diggs told me. He called me. He wants to know what you want, and he wants to be left alone."

"Diggs called you? Why you?"

A look of subdued surprise came to his eyes. "I'm his accountant," he said. "Didn't you know?"

"I hadn't gotten around to that yet."

"You would have eventually," he said. "It's hardly a secret that my practice consists of a number of small businessmen. Diggs happens to be one of them."

That answered the question of how Diggs knew I had been married to Norm Colquist's sister. It might also have provided answers to some other questions, if only I knew what the questions were. One thing I felt certain of. It wasn't as simple as Talent wanted to make it. He tried to toss off his connection to Diggs as one of those little coincidences that happen all the time. Sure. About as often as the neck bone is directly connected to the shinbone.

Norm Colquist and Elinor Garcia; Elinor Garcia and Ray

111

Diggs; Ray Diggs and Harold Talent. Coincidence, my foot.

Talent spoke, finally getting around to what he had really come to tell me. "Diggs says he wants no trouble. He says he doesn't have any information that will help you and you're wasting your time. He also threatens to sue you if you don't leave him alone."

"All right, you've delivered the message. Now here's another. Tell Diggs he's going to have to talk to me sooner or later, because that's the only way he can get me off his back."

"I see," said Talent. He leaned back in his chair. "Perhaps I could act as a go-between, arrange an accommodation that would serve both your interests."

"Maybe," I said. "What do you have in mind?"

"I could ask him the questions you would ask him and relay his answers to you."

"Assuming there were any answers."

"You mean he might prove reticent."

"So far," I said, "he's even refused to comment on the weather."

"He's afraid."

"I don't see that changing."

"Perhaps," said Talent, "if you would tell me your questions, in their context."

"You mean, tell you what I know so far."

"Yes. He might respond, if he saw no danger in it to himself. Do you have an alternative plan?"

"Not at the moment," I admitted. "All right. To start with, Norm didn't kill that woman. Someone else did, and Norm took the heat. It was meant to look like Norm had taken the Garcia murder weapon with him, but he didn't. It was planted on the body." I pushed my plate away. The omelet was cold, and I had lost my appetite. "Do you do Diggs's income taxes?"

He considered the question before answering. "Yes, of course. Why do you ask?"

112

"Elinor Garcia took an interest in Diggs's business and ran a file on him. Nothing in the file looked bad for him, but she may have known something she kept in her head instead of on paper. Now you come to say you're his accountant. Does all the stuff he turns over to you add up?"

His eyes narrowed, searched my face. "Yes, it does."

"It would," I replied. "Probably there's not a quarter unaccounted for."

"What are you getting at, Broder?"

"Four things stand out. One, Diggs has friends in the mob who want him left alone. Two, he runs a string of businesses whose take is totally cash. Three, Elinor Garcia gets cozy with Diggs. Four, Elinor Garcia gets herself blasted."

"I see no connection."

"I think that Diggs's business involves laundering more than just clothes."

He thought that over for a moment. He said, "Money laundering? For gangsters?" His voice held a note of shock.

"That's right. And you're his accountant."

"Are you implying I would get mixed up with anything like that?"

"Hard to believe you wouldn't know about it. You could avert your eyes, of course. Like the genteel lady conversing with the man whose fly is open. You might not want to admit you had seen it, but you'd know."

Talent's glance dropped to the tabletop. "The Diggs accounts are not all they should be," he admitted. He reached for his glass. "Perhaps," he said, "I should suggest that Mr. Diggs find himself another accountant." He drank from his glass. "You have reason to think a connection exists between Diggs and Elinor Garcia?"

"Yes. I'm not sure, but it fits with everything else. Elinor Garcia, sharp young hustler, finds out, I don't know how, but let's assume she did. She wants a cut for keeping her mouth shut. Diggs finds himself in the middle. He can't divert any of the money to Garcia to keep her quiet, and he's afraid to

113

tell anyone inside the mob that she's blackmailing him."

"Because she found out about it from him?"

"I don't know and maybe Diggs doesn't either. But he can't be sure how she found out, and he's taking no chances."

"So he kills her."

"No. Diggs isn't acting like a killer, more like a killee. But he may know who did, or at least why she had to die. Diggs is scared, maybe because he thinks he could be next in line after Garcia."

"Yes," said Talent. A thoughtful expression came to his face. "Definitely Mr. Diggs must find a new accounting firm."

"Not until you ask him some questions," I said and reminded him of his offer to act as go-between. "Or find out where he is so I can ask him."

Talent suddenly stood up. "No. I want no part of this. I have my business and my family to think of. I warned you, Broder. I warned you to leave it alone, but you wouldn't. You had to keep going, to impress Margaret. Now look where it has led: to gangsters, to killers. You—"

"Sit back down, Talent. Things are going to get worse."

"What do you mean?"

"When I catch up to Diggs, he'll tell me just how far into this you are."

"No," he said. "I have no part of it."

"No? Then how did you find out Shaeffer was once on the take?"

He dropped his air of feigned innocence. He sat down. His stare probed my face. "So Shaeffer lied when he said you had agreed to drop the case."

"He didn't have much choice. He had to get you off his back until he could get Alvera to scare me off."

Talent's face turned to a bland mask. "Alvera?"

"If you're lucky," I said, "you don't know him. If you're unlucky, he knows you. I had Shaeffer between a rock and a

114

hard place. At first I thought it might have been Diggs who called Alvera for help, but I don't think so now. I think Diggs may be more afraid of Alvera than he is of me. It was Shaeffer who brought Alvera into it. Shaeffer couldn't shake me off by himself. He needed help, big help. He must have figured no one would buck Alvera."

Talent shook his head. "I had nothing to do with that."

"But you did lean on Shaeffer. You used what you knew about Shaeffer's background to force him to stonewall me on the Garcia case. You found out about Shaeffer's payoffs from someone in the Diaz mob. It was the only way. You have some of that same mud on your own shoes."

"Let it alone, Broder." His voice carried a clear warning. "You don't know what you're doing. You're blundering around, making life difficult, making enemies."

"Tell me about it. And tell me how it connects with Elinor Garcia's murder—and with Norm's."

He didn't respond to my request. Instead he said, "You and I could have lived both our lives without ever meeting each other."

"Except that Norm Colquist came to me on the night Elinor Garcia died."

"Yes. A mistake, that." He hid whatever else he thought about Norm's coming to see me behind an impenetrable stare. "That and Margaret's action in going to you. I suppose I always knew she would, someday."

"Leave her out of this, Talent. This thing is between you and me. She hasn't anything to do with it."

"She may have everything to do with it."

For a moment our eyes locked glances. Then he stood up. "I'll talk to Diggs for you. Perhaps something can be arranged that will satisfy you without ruining too much of the furniture."

"It's getting late," I said. "Don't take too long."

I had two whiskeys after he left and sat for a long time

115

thinking about what he had said. I didn't like what I was thinking. It had to do too much with where Talent stood with people who were friends and associates of Manny Diaz. Innocent bystanders were known to get in the way when the bullets start flying. Maybe my fears were groundless, but I had them anyway, and I couldn't just sit around doing nothing about them.

I stood up and went to the pay phone and called the Talent home. Margaret answered. Talent had not returned home. She didn't know where he was or when he would come back.

I told her he had come to see me. "I think you should get out, Margaret. Pack up and leave, tonight."

She didn't understand and she reminded me of what I had said earlier. "You told me I should come back here."

"I was wrong. I didn't know then what I know now," I replied. "He's mixed up with people who hurt other people. I don't know how far in he is, but it could get bad."

"You said it would. We've already talked about that."

"I didn't realize then how bad."

"These other people, you mean."

"That's right."

"Why would they want to hurt me?"

"I don't know that they would. But it's better for you to be out of harm's way, you and the children."

"I sent the children down to Venice with friends for a few days. I need time alone to sort things out."

"Join them. Sort things out with long walks on the beach."

"I can't. Harold brought Norman's body back today. There are arrangements to be made. Things—"

"Let your husband make the arrangements."

"There's a memorial service tomorrow. I have to be there. I'm his only family, Paul."

"All right," I said. "One night. After the service tomorrow, get out."

"If you say it's necessary, I'll go."

"It may not be necessary, but it's smart."

116

"All right," she agreed. "Tomorrow."

I took a deep breath and let it out. Tomorrow was better than nothing. If I'd had anything to go on other than vague concerns, I'd have insisted on her leaving sooner. But I didn't, and I had to admit she was looking at it from a more practical viewpoint than I was. However, she needed to know one more thing.

I said, "Talent has a lot on his mind. He's drawn pretty tightly." I let it go at that.

"If you are suggesting that I avoid him . . ." she began. She paused noticeably. "We've had separate bedrooms for some time. Long before Norman disappeared. Ever since—" She cut herself off in mid-statement. "It's not important. Harold and I understand each other now. I can deal with him."

Maybe she could handle the Harold Talent *she* knew. She sounded sure enough. What bothered me was whether she could handle the Harold Talent *I* was beginning to know.

"Margaret," I said, "I could quit; you know, give it up."

"And put everything back the way it was?"

I made no reply. I couldn't put everything back in its place, of course, and there was no point pretending I could.

"You see?" she went on. "We've opened too many doors. You told me that. And we have. We've opened doors that look in on other people's secrets. Doors that look in on our own secrets." She paused. "If I go, will you keep me informed of what's going on?"

"Yes, of course. One more thing, Margaret. Norm was in Gamblers Anonymous several years ago, wasn't he?"

"Yes. After he lost heavily and asked us to help him pay off his debts. Why?"

"In a moment. Now think carefully about this. When did you realize he had begun to gamble again?"

She didn't answer right away. In the background I could hear music, old stuff, soft and mellow.

She spoke. "I don't think I was ever aware of it, not until he left. Now that I think back, I never realized he had started to gamble again. And I should have, shouldn't I?"

"Yes. I don't think he could have been gambling heavily without your knowing it." I told her about Norm's friend from Gamblers Anonymous. "Norm lied about his gambling debts."

"But he called Harold to ask for money."

"That was part of the lie. And those calls bring up another interesting question. How did Norm know where to call if he didn't ask you, seeing as he and Talent were barely speaking?"

"You have it wrong, Paul. Harold never liked Norman, but those feelings didn't prevent Norman from working with him."

What I knew of the feelings between Talent and Norm Colquist came from the two of them, each with his own reason to lie, each with his own track record of doing it. In Margaret, however, I had a witness in a position to know the truth and to tell it.

"Tell me about it," I suggested.

"I never asked about the specifics," she said. "I believe Norman cashed checks and made deposits and occasionally established bank accounts for new businesses. I understood Norman was working off his old gambling debt, the one Harold paid for him several years ago."

"So it's possible your husband himself told Norm where he would be that Sunday night."

She said, "I suppose so. Does it make a difference?"

"I wish I knew."

"What now?" she asked.

"There's a man I have to find tomorrow," I told her. "Before his friends discover I'm still looking for him."

The phone woke me. I was sitting in a chair in the living room of my rented beach place, a bottle of Dewars on the table beside me. The drive back from Tampa had given me a false sense of full wakefulness. I made a drink and sat down

118

to watch some television, a sure prescription for sleep. I had no idea how long I had been sleeping: an hour at least, maybe two.

I stood up and turned off the television and went to the kitchen. I took the wall phone and put it to my face and said, "Yes?"

"Broder?" asked an unfamiliar man's voice. I said yes again, and the voice said, "I got your message. I want to talk."

"Who is this?" I asked.

"The name is Diggs, Ray Diggs."

10

I STOOD FOR a moment, unsure of what to say, while my mental circuits came together. Finally I said, "My message. You've talked to Talent."

"That's right, but I don't like go-betweens. Do you want to talk or not?"

"Yes," I replied. "I want to talk to you about Elinor Garcia."

"You're trying to get us both killed, Broder."

"Like Garcia?"

Silence. Then, "I want to talk deal."

I asked, "What kind of deal?"

"I tell you what I know, but you make damn sure you let everybody know you got your information from somebody else."

"Is that what Talent suggested?"

"Fuck Talent. I'm sick of his bullshit. I'll fix it with him, but for now I'm doing what I think is best for me. You want to deal or not?"

"I'll deal," I said. "Who killed Elinor Garcia?"

"I'm not sure."

"But you have an idea. Was it Alvera?"

"Could be. Talent said you figured Garcia got wise to me running organization money through my laundromats. He said you were just guessing."

"Is that what Garcia found out, that you were laundering money as well as clothes?"

He hesitated before replying. "I think so. She never came right out and said so, but I think she knew."

"Tell me about it."

"Do we have a deal?"

"I want to see what I'm dealing for. What about Garcia?"

"Yeah," he replied. "It was like this, Broder. I'd never seen her before. One day she comes into one of the laundromats and says she's a management consultant, she puts deals together. She thought she could do something with the laundromat business and wanted me to help her learn something about the business."

"Why you?"

"Yeah, why me. Why the hell do you think? She knew something was going on and she wanted to get the whole bundle, probably so she could buy her way in."

"And you gave her the bundle, all about the operation."

Diggs breathed heavily over the phone. "Shit, Broder. As far as I knew at first, she was on the level. It wasn't until later, when she started asking about some of my suppliers, that I began to get a queasy feeling."

"Phony suppliers. People you funneled mob money to."

"That's right," he replied. "But what the hell did I know? I don't take care of that end. Hell, man, she came up with the names of businesses I never heard about. She was way ahead of me."

"But you talked to her."

He hesitated, and the silence was filled by a heavy roaring sound in the background, like that of a tractor-trailer rig. He was probably calling from a pay phone near a highway. The roar receded as he spoke again.

"She let me know I was in for a treat if I helped her. Jesus, I'd have told her anything to get into her pants. At my age, I never figured I'd ever have a shot at anything like her again."

I wondered if he had explained all that to Mary Alice, but I kept it to myself. Aloud, I said, "And you're scared she told somebody what she knew and how she knew it. Somebody in the mob, maybe, when she went looking for a piece of the action."

121

"She didn't get it all from me, but I guess she got something. If she told anybody how she found out, I'd be dead meat by now. I'd be in the bay with a a truck wheel tied to my ankles and a plastic bag over my head."

"Alvera."

"Yeah. Look, Broder. Tommy used to come in the Shadows plenty when I worked there. He's nuts. Mr. Diaz can control him, but nobody else can. When the old man's gone, Tommy's going to want to take over, and he's going to be settling some old scores. He'll want to seem like the one guy who was looking out for the organization while the old man was sick. He's going to be looking for people to shoot."

"The cops won't like that."

Diggs snorted over the phone. "What the hell good is that going to do the dead guys, even if the cops do pin anything on him? Four people I know of who've crossed Tommy in the last couple of years have been fished out of Tampa Bay, and one out of the Hillsborough River, and Tommy's still riding around town in that big white Lincoln."

"What do you want me to do?"

"Meet me tonight. After that I'm leaving town for a week. While I'm out of town, you keep on investigating like you don't know squat. We'll set up somebody else to take the blame, make it look like anything you found out came from somebody else. I'll be in the clear when I get back."

"But you'll give it all to me tonight?"

"Do we have a deal?"

I thought it over. If Garcia had stumbled onto a money-laundering operation and had died as a result of it, that would do for the reason I needed to go over Shaeffer's head and have the case reopened. On the other hand, a lot could happen in a week. Talent could find out that Diggs had gone off on his own, disregarding Talent's advice. Alvera could learn that Diggs had talked. And Shaeffer wouldn't sit still for a week.

A week was a long time, but I saw no other choice. First I

122

had to have the information, and tonight looked like my last chance to get it.

"All right," I agreed. "We have a deal. But I have to know who the someone else is, the guy who's going to take the fall for you talking. We need somebody in a position to know."

"I have someone in mind," said Diggs. His voice sounded grim. "You'll understand when you get it all."

"All right." I was ready to take his word for it. I had to let him do it his way. "Wait'll I get a pencil and paper. I want every detail."

"Not over the phone," said Diggs, his voice definite. "My old hotel room at the Imperial Palm, four forty-five. Last place anybody'd figure for me to meet you."

"Alvera may have men watching it," I pointed out.

"Don't worry. I can get in without anyone seeing me."

"Including the guy at the desk?"

"Yeah. Including him." He paused, probably to look at his watch. "Can you make it by midnight?"

I said I could, and we arranged to meet at the locked rear door that faced the alley in back of the hotel.

"One more thing," I said before we hung up. "Did Garcia tell Norm Colquist what she found out?"

I meant the question to confirm what logic had already pointed to. It made sense to assume that Elinor Garcia would have told Norm about her discovery, because they were lovers. In that situation, even a tight-lipped woman might loosen up, especially if her lover needed money. And Norm always needed money, even when he wasn't gambling.

The pieces began to fit. He must have known about her murder. The lie about his gambling debts would extend to the story about the men waiting for him in front of his apartment. There was nothing to stop him from going into his apartment that evening and finding her body. That gave him two good reasons for fleeing: one, that he'd be blamed for killing her and, two, that he'd be next.

No wonder he had been so scared. He would have known

what it had meant, that she had to die because of what she knew about the mob's money-laundering operation and that he knew just as much.

I repeated my question. "She told Colquist, didn't she?"

"You got it all wrong, Broder," replied the heavy-winded man on the other end of the line. "He was the jerk who let it slip to her." And the phone went dead.

So much for logic.

I splashed cold water on my face from the kitchen faucet and made a cup of instant coffee for the road. I flipped off the light switch in the kitchen and picked up the coffee mug and started for the living room. Something stopped me: a feeling, maybe, a tingling at the base of my neck. Or was it something more substantial? When I turned out the light, I had glanced automatically out of the kitchen window. My brain had registered something out there, something out of place.

The window in the kitchen faced toward the alley. I wanted a better look at that alley, but I didn't want to be backlighted by the light coming from the living room. The kitchen had a swinging door. I closed it, shutting off the light from behind me. I put the coffee mug on the counter and returned to the window.

I gave my eyes a moment to become accustomed to the darkness. I stood a little to the side of the window, just enough so that I could look around the café curtains. Like all the other windows, the kitchen window had glass jalousies, dating the building back to the fifties. You don't see glass jalousies much anymore.

I peered out. I saw three cars parked along the opposite side of the alley. Two of them were familiar. The third, a dark four-door sedan of indeterminate make, sat in the shadows to my right, its occupants, if any, hidden behind solar-black windows.

My eyes searched the street to my left. Three seconds

later, I saw the shadow I expected to see. He was standing close to a tall palmetto bush, half obscured by its foliage.

I retreated from the window a step and sorted out the alternatives. I discarded almost immediately the possibility that the police had staked out my place, because they had no reason to do it. That left Alvera and his boys, which raised a big question in my mind. Had the phone call from Diggs been a setup? To make sure that I was home? That didn't make sense. The call had come only minutes earlier, nowhere nearly enough time for Alvera's gunnies to drive over from Tampa.

No. They had come earlier and had been waiting out there. But for what? For me to sleep? They might make a move then. Or for me to leave? They'd have another car, perhaps, farther up the island, to block the street. With a car behind me and one in front of me, they'd have me trapped. Into one of those cars I'd go, at gunpoint. And then there would be a plastic bag over *my* head and the truck wheel at *my* ankles. Over the side of the Bayway I'd go, to the bottom of Boca Ciega Bay.

Nice thought. The telephone didn't give me time to dwell on it. Its ringing, loud in the night stillness, summoned me back to it. I answered. It was Shaeffer on the other end.

He spoke with cold purpose in his tone. "Talent called me," he said. "He told me tomorrow will be my last day as a police officer. That's because you told him everything."

"He has his back to the wall."

"Tell me about it, you sonofabitch."

"I think he's involved in money laundering."

"You think? Tell me what you know, Broder, not what you think."

"Ray Diggs knows about it. You remember Ray Diggs, don't you? The guy you said was clean?"

"That doesn't help me," he replied.

"Maybe it would, if you knew what Diggs knows."

"Which is what?"

"I won't know it all until I talk to him. Then maybe I can do something for you. Maybe I can do something for us both."

"Listen, Broder, you tell me where he is, and I'll talk to him. I'll do something. You just get the fuck off this case."

"So that you can pull the cover over the Garcia killing and make Talent happy?" I paused. "No."

A long silence over the telephone. Then, "I hear Alvera doesn't like it that you're still looking for Ray Diggs."

"Let me guess how Alvera found out," I said. "I tell Harold Talent I want answers from Diggs. Talent tells you I'm still on the case and your ass is in the frying pan because of it. Only way you know to get your ass to a cool place is to tell Alvera to scare me off. That about right?"

He gave it a second's thought before speaking. "Not quite," he said, his voice grim. "You left a trail, Broder. Alvera picked it up. It wasn't me. I made a mistake in thinking I could use Alvera as an errand boy. Yeah, I tipped him off about Diggs after I knew you were going after Diggs. That was okay then, because he doesn't like you. I don't know why."

"I do. Tommy and I go back a long way. I'm surprised he didn't do what you asked him to do, which was to put me out of the way permanently. Right?"

"That would be best for everybody."

"Everybody but me," I said. "So what went wrong?"

"What went wrong," he replied, "is that I don't know what in the hell is going on. Tommy called *me* this time. He's curious. He wants to know what it is with you and Diggs. I tell him you're just investigating the Garcia thing, and he doesn't believe me. He wants to know things I can't tell him."

"About what I want from Diggs? And where Diggs is?"

"That's right. Look, Broder, some people say Tommy Alvera missed getting all his upstairs parts wired, but I can tell you he's not stupid. He knows something's going on."

"And he wants in on it."

126

"That's right," he said. He paused, and added, "Why don't you take a vacation. Just get in your car and go. If you don't, somebody's going to kill you."

"Yeah," I said. "Maybe somebody will. And it looks like they've already arrived."

The problem with my place was that there was no back door or window. There are windows on the front and on one side, the bedroom side. Whoever was in the car had the front in view, and the guy by the palmetto bush could see both the bedroom side and the front. They had me bottled up. I knew it, and they maybe thought they knew it. I had to make them begin to doubt it.

I opened the door between the kitchen and the dining ell and went out to the living room. The men across the alley probably realized I had been looking out from the darkened kitchen. They had to assume they had been spotted, which was okay with me. It would make everything I planned to do seem to them just the way I wanted it to look.

With the kitchen light off, only the two living-room lamps remained lit. I extinguished both. The interior of my cottage slid into total darkness.

I returned to the bedroom and went to the side window and went to work on the glass jalousie.

Several slats of glass came out of the side holders with varying degrees of difficulty. Most, however, would not budge, and I needed enough of them out to make the window opening large enough for a body the size of mine. There was only one answer. Several sharp blows with the .38 shattered the glass. The noise of its breaking sounded loud in the stillness of the night and must have reached the watchers across the alley. It gave the whole charade a nice touch of authenticity. Then I tore out the window screen.

I went around the bed and took the .45 automatic from its place on the nightstand. In my opinion, they haven't made a better firearm for close-in work, especially in the dark. I

127

stuck it in my belt and went to the kitchen and tapped out the number of my answering service on the phone buttons and told the voice that answered, "Call me in ten minutes. Let the phone ring twelve, fifteen times. Ten minutes, exactly. Got it?"

She had it.

I went into the living room. There was a light outside, under the little roof that stuck out above the door. The switch was on the inside wall. I flipped the light on, and then off, almost immediately. In the dark, I pushed open the screen door and let it bang shut.

I went quickly into the closet and squeezed the closet door shut behind me. In the closet ceiling was the access panel to such attic as you are likely to find in low-roofed Florida houses. Usually there's room up there to store your luggage and a few other things.

I slid back the access panel and hoisted myself up, not an easy thing to do unless you're used to twenty-five chin-ups a day, and made even more difficult because I could not remove the closet shelf. I couldn't replace it once I was in the attic.

I have two suitcases and a small traveling bag up there on a piece of two-by-four-foot plywood. I pushed them aside, closed the access panel, and sat cross-legged in the warm still air with my head bent away from the roof rafters. While I waited, I pulled the .45 from my belt and laid it in my lap.

After a while, from what seemed a long way off, I heard the phone ring. I counted thirteen rings, but I may have missed one or two. And then it stopped, as though no one were at home to answer it. My watchers outside must have been feeling a little uneasy.

I had not long to wait after that. I thought I heard the front door slam closed, then voices. The closet door beneath me opened and the voices were plainer.

"Shit," said one. "He must have gone out the fucking window. And you," he said to someone, probably the man I had seen standing beside the palmetto bush, "were supposed to be watching the side."

"I was, dammit," said another voice. "But it was dark, and then he started cocking around with the front lights and screen door."

"So you took your goddam eyes off the real thing while Broder put on a show for you," said the first voice. "Tommy's going to shit his pants."

"It wasn't my fault. Maybe I took a quick look at the front door, but just for two seconds, that's all. No way he could have got out that window so fast."

"Sure," said the first voice, its tone heavy with sarcasm. "He just turned fucking invisible, that's what. Shit, let's get back to Tampa and tell Tommy and get it over with. Jesus, what a night!"

Silence fell, broken in a few moments by the sound of a car engine starting, followed by the sound of tires gouging crushed seashells from the alley's surface.

I slid open the attic panel and dropped down the small travel bag. Alvera's boys might return, and that could make the place at Pass-a-Grille unhealthy for future occupancy.

I walked up the alley to the rear of the Imperial Palm Hotel with my right hand inside my jacket. My fingers curled around the grip of the .38 as a precaution, but I didn't expect trouble. If Diggs had lied, if he had allied himself with Alvera to trap me, Alvera's men would not have come for me at Pass-a-Grille. Still, the .38 was a comfort in that dark alley.

Dark, that is, except for the single light bulb over the rear door to the Imperial Palm. The door itself was steel. It had no knob or handle of any kind on the outside. It fit snugly shut. I rapped quietly on it with two knuckles of my left hand. Nothing happened.

I looked at my watch. Two minutes past midnight. I knuckled the door again, and again no response of any kind came from the other side.

129

I retreated to the far side of the alley and stood in the darkness, in the shadow of some kind of steel shed. I waited for five minutes, for ten. The door did not open.

The questions began to come after fifteen minutes of waiting. Had Diggs changed his mind about meeting me? Had he told someone of his deal with me? Where was Ray Diggs? What had gone wrong?

I wasn't sure where I could find the answers to my questions, but I didn't figure to find them in the alley behind Diggs's hotel. I walked the two blocks back to my car and took the bag out of the trunk and went in search of a taxicab.

The cabbie, at my direction, made one slow pass along the street in front of the Imperial Palm. I gave each of the two dozen or so cars parked in that block careful scrutiny. I saw none that I recognized or any that looked suspicious. We circled the block and pulled up in front of the Imperial Palm. I paid the driver and headed inside with my travel bag.

I had to ring the front bell and wake up the night desk man in order to get in. He had not seen me before. I said to him, "What I need is a quiet room and a good night's sleep."

He slid a registration card across the counter, and I filled it out in the name of Bill Downs of Miami Springs and pushed it back with the cash to cover one night's stay. He gave me change and a key and said, "Second floor, front."

I went up in the elevator and went to my room and deposited my bag on the bed and returned to the elevator and rode it to the fourth floor and found room 445. The door was ajar, so I pushed it open with my elbow and went in.

A man lay on the floor, and the man fit Ray Diggs's description. A good part of his blood lay on the floor beside him, more of it than he could afford to lose. Ray Diggs had fallen there, probably shocked into unconsciousness by the impact of the bullet holes in him, and had bled to death.

I glanced around the room for clues, but if there were any of the subtle variety they went overlooked. Time did not permit more than a quick glance. For all I knew, the cops could

130

already have been summoned and were on their way. The cops knew, or at least one of them knew, that I was looking hard for Ray Diggs and that when I found him I planned to lean on him.

I gave his lifeless corpse one more glance. I didn't want Shaeffer to think I had leaned on him *that* hard. Shaeffer might like it too much. He might persuade his buddies in blue to reach the same conclusion, especially if they found me standing over the body. I was definitely in the wrong place at the wrongest possible time, so I did the only sensible thing.

I got the hell out of there.

I sat on the bed in Bill Downs's room and considered the situation. First came gratitude for having a room on the second floor right above the street. If the Tampa police force showed up, I didn't even have to look out the window to know about it. The flashing red and blue roof lights on the squad cars would shine into my window and the racket from their radios could easily penetrate the silence of my room.

The street was quiet, which made it seem like a good time to get out of the Imperial Palm and look for another hotel in which to spend the night. I grabbed my bag and went out to the hall and found the stairs and walked down to the lobby. If my luck had anything good left about it at all, the desk clerk would have once more fallen asleep, and I didn't want the noisy elevator waking him up.

As it turned out, he was nowhere in sight. If that was unusual, I let it pass, glad of the opportunity to get out without being seen. I opened the front door silently and stepped out into the peaceful night air. I crossed the deserted street quickly and turned right.

A man stepped out of a hedge. He wore a white sport jacket with an *M* embroidered over the pocket. He held a gun pointed at my midsection. "Hold it, Broder," he said.

From behind me came footsteps, and a hard object rammed into my ribs. "Hands," said a voice. I obeyed, and

131

the man behind me snapped handcuffs on my wrists.

"Let's go," Max said and smiled coldly in the uncertain light. "Alvera wants to talk to you."

11

WE DROVE TO an area near the docks, with me in the back seat with my travel bag and Max turned so he could keep his eye on me over the back of the front seat. The black, empty eye that was the muzzle of his gun stared at me. Max also had my gun.

Neither of them wanted to talk to me. After an initial attempt on my part to get them to tell me why Alvera was so interested in me, we lapsed into silence.

The driver went through downtown Tampa on Kennedy and headed toward the docks, on the other side of the channel. When we stopped it was in front of a truck-loading platform attached to what looked like a warehouse. Max and his gun came to my side of the car.

He said, "Out," and I got out, because he added, "Alvera said to kill you if you gave us any trouble."

The two of them, both with guns drawn, marched me across the pavement and up five concrete steps at the end of the loading platform and into the building and through a maze of crates and bales piled high. The air was hot and still and thick.

We came to a door. Max opened it, and we passed through a short corridor with office cubicles on either side to another door. It had a simple knob lock, the kind you can always exit but need a key for entering. Max used a key.

About six feet distant was another door, set into a cinder-block wall. The door was made of heavy planks running horizontally. A rough two-by-six-inch plank barred the door. One end of the plank was bolted into the cinder-block wall on one side of the door. The other end rested in a steel bracket bolted to the wall on the other side of the door.

On each side of the door, a small board nailed to the door assured that the bar, when lowered into position, would hold the door snugly. It left a gap of an inch or slightly less between the bar and the door but guaranteed that no prisoner could rattle the cage door.

Max lifted the end of the plank that rested in the steel bracket and swung the plank upward. It pivoted on the bolt through the other end. He swung it up and clear of the door and pulled the door open.

A twin-tubed fluorescent light fixture on the ceiling bathed the room beyond in cool white light. The man behind me pushed me in with a shove against the small of my back.

I stood in a small, square room. There were no windows in the spray-enameled cinder-block walls. For furniture, I saw only an aluminum camp cot and a small table and chair. A bucket stood on the floor near the table, another in the far corner. The one in the corner had a round wooden lid.

Max said, "On the chair, Broder."

I went to the chair and sat down and started trying to figure a way to get out of there. Neither Max nor his partner said anything.

After five minutes of waiting, when I still hadn't come up with an answer, Tommy Alvera walked in. He stood for a moment just inside the door, eyeing me. Then he walked across the floor, his shoes making little tapping sounds on the concrete. He held a cigar in his left hand. He put his right hand in his trousers pocket and rattled his coins.

He said, "You don't listen good. You were told to stay clear of Ray Diggs." He puffed on his cigar, his eyes black and cold: hard eyes yet strangely blank, seemingly devoid of thought.

"I'm not looking to cause trouble," I said.

"Yeah? Then why are you still bothering Ray Diggs?"

"Who said I was bothering him?"

Alvera dragged deeply, contentedly, on his cigar and exhaled a mouthful of smoke, which expanded to a bushel-sized cloud and hung in the quiet air of the little room, dissipating slowly. "So what were you doing in his hotel?"

"It was Diggs's idea."

"Yeah? Why?"

"He wanted to talk about Elinor Garcia," I said.

"Where is the sonofabitch now?"

"In his room at the Imperial Palm. At least that's where I left him."

"Max," ordered Alvera. "See about it."

"Won't do any good," I said. "He's dead."

Alvera took the cigar from his mouth and stared at me. "Did you kill him?"

"No. Did you?"

He ignored the question. "Max, call the hotel. Find out if Diggs is dead." Max went out of the room, and Alvera turned his blank eyes back to me. "You think you're a tough sonofabitch. I'll see how much you can take before you talk."

"Whatever I have to, Tommy. The way I look at it, you won't let me out of here alive after I tell you what I know. That means the longer I hold out, the longer I live."

He put his cigar back in his mouth and chewed it silently. "All right," he said at last. "I don't have all night, so I'll give you a break. You talk, you walk." He puffed again. "It's like this, Broder. The old man is going fast. He may not last the night. Right now, a lot of people think that Al Connor is the best man to take over."

"You don't agree."

"I'm taking over, any way I can. That means some of Al's people are going to wind up in the bay, maybe Al too. Me, I don't give a fuck one way or the other, but if I could make Al look bad to the old man now, I wouldn't have to worry about putting Al away until after the old man gets a decent burial."

"How do you plan to make Connor look bad?" I asked.

135

"Diggs works on Al's side of the organization. Al persuaded Manny to set up a fancy deal to make the two of them look legitimate. It's all bullshit to me, but Al likes to hang around with stockbrokers and bankers. And Manny, at the time Al came up with the idea, was getting old. He started to worry about dying and maybe not being allowed to get planted in holy ground. You know, that church shit."

From outside the room, I could hear footsteps on the concrete floor approaching and then the sound of a telephone ringing, and the footsteps stopped coming and receded once more into the silence.

Tommy Alvera continued. "So now Al's operation ain't working so good. Things are going wrong. I know enough about it to see that, but you know more. I want to know what you know. Okay, so you and I never got along, but the way I look at it, we can still deal."

"It's hard to deal when all the guns are on one side."

He nodded his head. "Yeah, but look at it from where I sit. I can't give your gun back to you now. Shit, you might start using it. I couldn't blame you none, I guess, but look where that would get us." He looked around to the other man, the one who had driven the car. Alvera said, "Put that goddam thing away, Tony."

Tony stuck his cannon into his shoulder holster and buttoned his jacket across it and stood with his arms folded.

Alvera looked back to me. "Okay," he said. "No guns. Now, what the hell is going on?"

I gave them each a look. They were still two against one, and they still had all the guns, even though none were pointed at me. Besides, I was sitting in a chair with handcuffs on my wrists, and I didn't know when Max would return. Agreeing to Alvera's offer seemed my best bet.

I held out my wrists behind me and rattled the handcuffs. "What about these?"

It turned out that Max had the key and Tommy was in a hurry. He didn't want to be the missing man when Manny

Diaz breathed his last. If I held out too long, what I knew would lose its value, both to Tommy and to me.

"Elinor Garcia was a smart girl on the hustle," I said. "She learned enough from Norm Colquist to make her suspicious of Ray Diggs's laundromat business. Since both she and Norm are dead, we will never know what he told her or how much Norm knew about the money laundering."

"She found it out from Diggs?" Alvera asked, expelling cigar smoke. "Then he killed her?"

"He said not. He thought it was one of your boys."

The black eyes blinked once. "Me? Shit, I only heard about the woman after she was shot. Why the hell would I do it?"

"No reason," I said, "if you never heard of her." I was skeptical but in no position to argue with him. "Suppose she took her story to someone else in the organization and demanded a piece of the action in return for her silence?"

"Nobody could be so stupid, Broder. And you say that she was a smart girl." He shook his head. "How'd she get it?"

"Five bullets in the chest and gut in Norm Colquist's apartment."

"You don't figure that's the way I'd do it, do you?"

"No. You'd tell her that the money was ready for her, and you'd set up a meeting. The meeting would take place in a house in a quiet family neighborhood. The guy who owned the house would go along because he owed you a favor or because he was afraid of you. The victim would arrive scared and ready for a trick but the family would be there, kids and all. The victim would relax and go into another room, not knowing that the family would be going to the movies soon. Next time anyone sees the victim is when the cops fish a body out of the bay with a plastic bag over the head and a truck wheel tied to the ankles."

"You know," he said, "you could be too damn smart for your own good."

"You asked," I replied. "But if you didn't kill her, then

137

who did?" I didn't expect an answer, and I didn't get one. "Now Diggs gets it in the same way as Garcia."

"Lots of people walking around with guns these days."

"Uh-huh, but usually a person has to have a good reason before pulling the trigger. Unless Garcia threatened to expose the money-laundering operation to the cops, I don't see any reason. If she did, you guys had the reason."

"Shit. That's it? That's all you got?"

"That's it." I decided to keep to myself what I knew about Harold Talent's role in the money laundering. Diaz or Connor might not be happy with me knowing so much. Of course, Alvera would be happy, because then he could tell everyone that he had found out and protected the organization from me. Just to prove it, you could look me up. In the bay.

"You're not much help," said Alvera. He scratched his cheek, trying to think through what he had been told. From outside the room came the sound of rapidly approaching footsteps. Max appeared in the doorway.

He said, "That was the house. The old man's going fast. If you want to be there for the end, you'd better hurry."

"Shit!" exclaimed Alvera. He looked around the room for some place to dispose of his cigar, found nothing, and handed it to Tony, who took it with a look of distaste on his face. Alvera said, "Take care of this for me. I gotta get up to the house. Shit." He headed for the open door. When he got there, he stopped and turned and asked Max, "What about Diggs?"

"Place was full of cops," replied Max, "according to the guy I talked to. They had an anonymous tip. Must have arrived about ten minutes after we took him." He jerked his head toward me.

Alvera turned his face toward me, his mouth curling into a cruel smile. "Sucker," he said. He looked at his two thugs. "Don't kill him while I'm gone, unless he gives you trouble." He paused on his way out to say, "Just beat the shit out of him."

As the sound of Alvera's footsteps in the outside hall faded, I gathered my feet under my center of gravity and pushed out of the chair, driving into Tony's gut with my shoulder. I had the satisfaction of getting two deep grunts out of him, but I hadn't much time to enjoy the feeling. A hard object seemed to split my skull, and bright flashing stars dropped into it.

When I awoke, dripping with water, my arms were above me. Instead of one pair of handcuffs, I now wore two, the other end of each being looped over an iron hook protruding from the wall above my head.

Max and Tony took turns on me. Max enjoyed it, especially the gut punching. He even said he enjoyed it. He took his time. He'd show me his fist and then drive it into my gut. I couldn't double over, stretched out the way I was. Max laughed.

When I sagged in my handcuffs, they took a short breather and doused me with more water. Max wrapped his fist in a towel so as not to hurt himself and hit me in the face. I tried to think of better days I've had, but after a while all I thought about was the pain. I don't know how long they worked on me. It seemed as though it would never end, but it did. It ended in the blessed blackness of unconsciousness.

I awoke to the sound of my own moaning. My cheek was pressed against the blanket that covered the thin foam mattress of the cot. I lay on my side.

I had coughed blood out onto the blanket, and its stickiness wet my cheek. I tried to open my eyes. One was swollen shut. The other could open only partway. The room was a blur.

I moved my arms and emitted an involuntary groan. After that I lay still for a long time, hoping for the return of unconsciousness. It didn't come back. I lay still. That way the pain was less.

But lying still provided no answer to my situation. Alvera

139

and his men would return. How often they returned depended on how much more my body could take and on how long they cared to keep me alive.

I got one eye open. My blurred view sharpened into focus. The eye saw no one in the room.

I tried to sit up. My head spun, making me sick. What I had to do I did into the bucket on the floor by the bed. At the time I didn't care how it came to be there. I had just time to throw off the round lid. The heaving in my gut created a new fountain of agony in my abdomen and rib cage.

I lay back on the cot, breathing heavily. My body said doing anything was impossible. My brain didn't agree.

"Up," I said quietly to the empty room. "Up, dammit, up."

I obeyed that command in stages. Sitting came first, then standing when I could. I walked—staggered, is more like it— to the little table. The bucket from which they had doused me stood there. It contained fresh water.

From each of my wrists dangled a pair of handcuffs. Each had an empty bracelet at the end. I dropped the empty bracelets at the end of my chains into the water, taking care not to allow them to hit the side of the bucket. I wanted no noise. I needed time, time to think and to do, before Max and Tony realized that I had regained consciousness.

I cupped my hands and splashed water on my face and head and neck. I straightened and let the water drip onto my shirt. Dried blood spotted it. I took a deep breath. No sudden spasm of pain resulted from the deep breath, and from that I concluded that none of my ribs were cracked. Bruised and painful, yes, but not broken.

I surveyed the room. There were only two openings in the walls, apart from the door. The air-conditioning vent near the ceiling was about six inches wide and a foot long. The return, near the floor, was maybe half again larger and covered with a heavy steel screen.

The only opening big enough for me was the door. I walked to it. It fitted snugly into its frame of two-by-eight-

140

inch planks anchored securely into the masonry walls. The door itself was constructed of the same thick planks, four of them running vertically. I seemed to remember, vaguely, that on the other side of the door the planks ran horizontally. That was two layers of planks. And that meant a solid wood door over three inches thick.

The door was hinged on the outside to swing outward. It had no handle on the inside. I pushed against it. It didn't budge. I remembered, more clearly now, that a two-by-six-inch plank barred the door on its other side. Max had had to lift the plank to open the door. At one end the the plank was bolted into the cinder-block wall and pivoted on that bolt. At the other end, when barring the door, it rested in a steel bracket bolted to the wall on the other side of the door.

At eye level for a short man, a hole about six inches by eight had been cut in the door. A varnished plywood panel closed off the opening. The panel seemed to have been built to slide open, but when I tried to open it, nothing happened. My fingers merely slid across the smooth varnish.

I limped back to the cot and sat on it and stared at the door with my one good eye. No matter how hard I stared, the door remained immovable.

My eye scanned the walls. It found no loose blocks, no disintegrating mortar. The only thing in the room close to disintegrating was me.

I stood up and limped around the concrete cell. No way out. There was no way out.

I stopped in the center of the room. Except the door. That was the only way. But the door had to be open. Like when Alvera's men returned.

It would be their two against my one, and the beating they had given me had robbed me of most of my strength. In addition, they had all the guns.

I had to take them unawares. Since the door opened outward, I would have no door to hide behind. Flatten myself against the wall, then.

141

"Sure," I said quietly to the room. "They'll just waltz right in. Sure they will."

The panel in the door had some function, like that of making sure the prisoner was where they could see him. If they could not see me when they slid back that panel, they would have a way of dealing with that. I wasn't the first person to occupy that room. They'd know what to do, from experience.

The cot was in plain view from the sliding panel, and they would expect to see me on the cot, hurting and afraid.

I went to the cot without hope and pulled back the mattress. The frame was light tubular aluminum. Attached to it were small springs all around the frame. In the middle, connected to the springs, thin metal slats ran crosswise and lengthwise. No weapon there. Nothing. I let the mattress flop back.

I leaned against the cold hard wall as a new wave of dizziness passed over me. I felt sick and loosened my belt. The sickness and dizziness passed, and I found myself sagging against the wall and sweating and holding onto each end of my belt as though to pull it apart.

The idea came through the curtain of pain. The door panel. "What the hell," I breathed almost silently.

What I needed was a pointed object to stick into the smooth plywood of the panel to open it. And I had such an object in my hand, the pin of my belt buckle. A little sharpening against the rough concrete floor and . . . well, I didn't know what I'd do when I got the panel open, but at least it was a start.

And an end. The damn thing wouldn't budge. They had even latched the panel.

I stopped, frozen in mid-movement by the faint sound of muffled voices on the other side of the door.

Alvera's men had arrived.

I headed back for the cot, hoping to buy time if they thought I was still unconscious. They would want me relatively fresh and alert. That's when fear sends its message more clearly; pain, its agony more intensely.

When the snap of the panel latch—that damned latch—reached my ears, my body curled into the fetal position on the cot. That's what they saw.

"Still out," said Tony's voice.

"Lemme take a look," said Max.

"Whatta you think?" asked Tony.

Go away, said the voice in my mind. A little more time, just a little more time.

I opened my good eye to a slit, hidden from them at that distance under the puffiness of the eye.

That's when I saw it. The belt. In my rush to return to the cot and feign continued unconsciousness, I had left the belt hanging on the door. Its buckle was caught in the slide track of the panel. If either of them looked a little to the side and straight down, he'd see it.

And if he saw it, they would know that I was faking.

I moaned quietly, hoping to keep Max's attention on me and away from where the belt buckle had become lodged.

Max said, "I think he's coming around. Let's have a beer and give him another twenty minutes."

Tony wasn't sure. "Suppose he wakes up and starts yelling?"

"You could set dynamite off in there and nobody'd hear it outside the warehouse. Besides, who the fuck'll hear him? There's only you and me here."

Tony said, "Yeah. Okay." Pause. The door panel slid back and forth. Then, "Shit, this thing is sticking. It'll close, but it won't latch."

I held my breath. If they explored the reason for the panel sticking, they'd find the belt and know that I was ready for more punishment. And that would be the end.

Max said, "Fuck it. Just shut the damn thing." The panel slid closed. I heard no click.

I exhaled and closed my one good eye and lay a moment

143

longer, letting the stillness of the room settle over me. Then I rose from the cot and went to the door. They had given me possibly twenty minutes, and the only thing I knew to do with it was to try to get that panel open. It had become a goal in itself, as though that tiny window to the outside could in some way lessen my confinement.

A notion formed itself in my mind. Twenty minutes would be plenty of time, if I could open the panel. That might allow me to put my arm through to the outside and reach down for the two-by-six plank that barred the door. I would attempt to raise it and open the door and slip out of the room and the warehouse unseen. The adrenaline began to pump as I thought about it. I felt a new burst of energy.

I took the belt buckle and worked its pin into a spot in the wood panel. I pushed on it. The panel slid open. Easy, easy.

That's when I saw the bars on the other side.

They were bolted to the outside of the door and set close together. To have any chance of grasping the plank that barred the door, I had to get my arm through the panel opening as far as my shoulder. I could get only my hand through the bars because of the handcuffs on my wrists. They formed a steel collar around the wrist too wide to pass through the narrow opening between the bars. I could get my arm through the bars only as far as my wrist. I could not reach the plank.

I withdrew my hand and stepped back and closed my eye and swore silently. Fatigue seeped into my body. I wanted to lie down, to rest. No time for that.

"Think," I told myself and opened my eye. "Have to move."

I went to the cot and looked down at it and ripped the mattress from it. I went to work on the springs with my fingers and managed to disengage two of the thin slats and one spring. I used the spring, which had a hook at each end, to join the two slats. I bent the end of one slat in the shape of a U and returned to the open panel in the door. I put the

144

two joined slats through the bars.

The idea was to hook the bent end of the slat under the plank on the outside of the door and lift it up.

My watch told me that nearly half the time I dared take had expired.

The feel of the slat sliding along the door, seeking the plank, transmitted itself to my hand. The hook of the slat caught the plank briefly, slipped, went past it.

I tried again. It caught again, and this time it held. I clutched the top slat with both hands and pulled. The sharp-edged slat cut my palms.

Then it gave way, but it wasn't the plank. I pulled up the slats. My fishing expedition had caught nothing. The bent end of the lower slat had not been strong enough and had straightened under the pressure. The plank fit too snugly to lift easily.

But that snug fit had been achieved at the expense of leaving a gap between the door and the plank that barred it. And that gap opened up a new possibility. If something could be gotten down through that gap and up the other side of the plank . . .

I discarded the bent slat. That left me with one slat and a spring. The spring had a hook at its free end, a hook to fish with. I returned to the door, belt in one hand and slat and spring in the other. I let the belt hand down, buckle at the lower end, along the outside surface of the door.

What I had to do was to snag the loop of the buckle with the hook on the spring at the end of the slat. Difficult, sure, but not impossible. I had three square inches of belt buckle opening to snag. When I snagged it, I would have a makeshift sling under the plank. It just took patience and time. I had plenty of the former, a shrinking margin of the latter.

I measured off the belt against the length of the slat and got both equal. That way I could avoid misses in the vertical direction. I held the tongue of the belt in my left hand and the slat in my right and began to maneuver the slat around where the belt buckle should have been. I needed only to move the hook of the spring back and forth until it engaged the belt buckle. Easy. Sure.

Thirteen minutes had been used up. I pulled my hook to see what I had snagged. Nothing. Again and again and again, nothing.

Sixteen minutes. I was running out of time.

My hands shook. Sweat oozed out of my palms. I took a deep breath and froze, straining to hear any sound. I thought I heard a sound but it was only my imagination, imagination fueled by fear.

I went fishing once more. Imagination that the slat felt an ounce heavier? No. God, no. The resistance increased as I lifted the slat. I had done it! I had snagged the belt buckle with the hook of the spring and now, as I raised the slat, the pressure grew as the spring extended. But it was a strong spring and its extension soon ended.

I had to wipe my hands. I held both ends of my sling with the numbing fingers of first one hand and then the other as I wiped my hands dry on my trousers. I couldn't let either end slip out of my sweating hands, not now. I had used eighteen minutes.

I clutched the ends of the sling, belt in one hand and slat in the other. I pulled.

I felt the plank rise. The belt slipped a little under the plank as it angled upward. I gathered in the belt and soon had the plank itself in my eager fingers. I pushed it higher, enough so that the door could open a little. The plank could not fall back into place now.

I opened the door and ran like hell.

Or at least as fast as I could.

12

I RAN AND then I walked, ducking and hiding at the approach of every pair of car headlights. I came to a lot of railroad tracks and had to avoid a slow-moving freight train. I saw nothing of Max and Tony, but I took no chances on trying to flag down any of those sets of approaching headlights I occasionally saw.

The area was built up, industrial, not without telephones. That's what I needed. As long as I had those handcuffs on my wrists, I doubted that any cabbie would stop for me, and I needed more reliable transportation than my legs.

I found a phone and a badly torn up Yellow Pages book outside of a tiny snack shop with paint peeling from its sides. No one previously had the same need for a locksmith as I did, so the page I needed was still in the book. I found the name I wanted and dialed. The number yielded a recording and a number to call in case of an emergency, which I considered applied to me. I dialed the second number. A man's voice answered.

"Art," I said. "It's Paul Broder."

Art's fuzzy voice said, "What? Broder?"

I said, "Wake up. I'm wearing bracelets that won't come off." And he said, "Uh. Yeah, Paul." He took a deep breath and let it out directly into the phone. "Where?"

I told him. I also needed some other things. "Stop at an all-night drugstore and bring me some bandages, antiseptic, and Tylenol." There was one other thing, too, but the liquor stores weren't open. "If you have any whiskey, bring that too."

A long half hour later he arrived, pulling up to the curb along the nearly deserted street. I limped across the sidewalk from my doorway and got into his car.

He said, "You need a doctor."

"I'll be okay," I said and extended my wrists. He had the handcuffs off in less than a minute.

"You can keep them," I said. I shook my hands, enjoying the feeling of freedom around my wrists. That freedom would not, however, last long if I returned to Pass-a-Grille. What I needed was a small motel where they wouldn't ask too many questions. "How about driving me to a motel? Over toward MacDill Air Force Base would be best, I think. Something cheap and not too particular. Someplace where I won't be the first guy to come in looking like he'd just been rolled."

"Cops or bad guys after you?" he wanted to know and I said, "Bad guys," and he nodded and drove me where I wanted to go and waited while I went inside.

The desk clerk gave a sharp glance to my bloodstained clothes and swollen, cut face.

I said, "It's a tough town," and he looked quickly away as he pushed the key across the counter to me.

I went back to Art's car, and he gave me a paper bag containing the things I had asked for. He said, "Vodka was all I had."

"That's fine," I said. "Put it on the bill too."

The eastern sky was turning pink as I crossed the parking lot and entered my room and sat down on the edge of the bed and closed my eyes and let out a deep breath.

I drank some vodka and brought ice back from the machine at the end of the building, and drank more vodka and took an extra long, extra hot shower that soothed some aches and opened some cuts to the cleaning action of soap and water. I dressed the cuts and put ice in a towel and held it over my eye. The vodka was beginning to catch up to me. I put the ice in the ice bucket and lay back on the bed. Sleep

148

came almost at once.

I awakened hungry and went naked into the bathroom and looked at the bruises on my body. They weren't nice, but the face looked the worst. Small strip bandages pulled together the two worst cuts. Thin lines of dried blood marked the minor ones. The eye was still swollen shut.

I needed to eat, but for that I needed decent clothes to wear out to a restaurant. No one would object to seeing a man who had taken a beating as long as he looked as though he had not come directly from it to breakfast. It would not be the closed eye and the bandages that were so objectionable, it was the blood on the clothes. That, nobody wanted to see, certainly not over pancakes and sausage.

The only thing to do was to get out of my comfortable nest and get some clothes and something to eat. I called a cab and told him to take me to the nearest Maas Brothers store. The clerk in the men's department looked at me with some distaste, but he got over that when he saw a two-hundred-dollar sale in the making. I exchanged my new threads for the old in the dressing room, stuffed my old clothes into a shopping bag, and put the bag into a litter can on my way to a late breakfast.

After that I called the answering service. Judy answered. "The police were here, looking for you. We had to give them the address and phone number of the Pass-a-Grille place."

"That's okay. Did they say what they wanted me for?"

"Paul . . . ," she began, hesitated, and went on. "They say you are wanted for murder and are armed and dangerous."

Shaeffer would like that, I thought. It gave him an excuse to shoot me. Something needed done about that, only I didn't know what. Get a lawyer and go to Tampa Street and surrender? Pray that nothing happened to me in my cell, and after that pray for acquittal? And if that didn't work out, pray the jury would recommend life instead of the chair?

Or leave town? Maybe Shaeffer would let me return after he got his pension. Maybe Alvera would forget me. And then

149

again maybe Shaeffer would have all the cops in the country looking for me, and when they found me he would tell Alvera where I was.

None of those possibilities appealed to me. I needed an alternative, and I didn't have one. Not yet, at any rate.

"Anything else?" I asked, my mouth dry.

"Margaret Talent called," she replied and gave me a number. "She said it was urgent."

I hung up and called the number Margaret had left. It wasn't her home phone.

She said, "Yes?" Her voice was cautious.

"It's me."

She breathed a deep sigh. "I'm glad you called," she said. "I'm leaving Tampa, Paul. I don't know when I'll come back."

"It's the right thing," I told her, wondering what had decided her, glad she'd be out of harm's way.

"Yes. I think so too." She paused. A moment of silence came between us before she spoke again. "Buy a girl a drink?" she said. "For old times' sake?"

For old times' sake. Her brother had used those words. Take care of her, will you, he'd asked, for old times' sake? I hadn't done a very good job of it. Or of taking care of myself, either.

I had a lot on my mind, but before she left, she needed to know the whole story on her husband, or as much of it as I knew. She had that much coming to her.

"I'd like that," I said. "Where are you?"

"At the airport Marriott," she replied. "I left home in rather a hurry, Paul, so I came here and took a room. I'll tell you about it when I see you. Where do you want to meet me? The lounge here? Bennigan's? Or someplace closer to town."

I thought about all the cops in Tampa who were out on the streets looking for me at that very moment. I said, "What's your room number?"

150

She let me into a room that was wide and deep and thickly carpeted. The room contained two double beds, both neatly made, table, chairs, and lamps.

Margaret wore a white sleeveless sweater and burgundy pants and slight bruise on her temple. Her expression turned from expectation to shock when she saw my face.

"Oh, God, Paul," she said.

"It's okay," I said. "Do you have any ice?"

She did, and she put it in a towel, and I sat on one of the chairs by the table. I held the towel of ice against my eye. She wanted to know what else she could do, and I said again that I was okay.

She said, "I've left him." She pulled the other chair out from the table and sat on the chair and looked across to me. "Early this morning. Last night, after he talked to you at that restaurant, we argued. He accused me of lying to him about you. I told him yes, because you were the only one who had helped Norman. He hadn't, not even when Norman pleaded with him. He said my brother was a fool and I should be glad he was out of my life. Then he accused me of sleeping with you. He said I was a slut. He hit me, two or three times. I ran into my bedroom and locked the door."

"Did he go out at all?"

She shook her head. "I don't know. All I did was lie curled up on the bed listening for any sound at the door. I didn't undress. I think I might have slept a little toward morning. Then I heard him at the door. He had a crowbar and was breaking the lock, splintering the side of the door. He came in. He said he was sorry to have neglected me but if I needed sex he would take care of it. I fought him off and ran away, out of the house to the neighbors' across the street. At daylight I went back and took my car. I had an extra key hidden behind the bumper. He didn't come out of the house." She breathed heavily, in and out. "I suppose I'll have to go back for my clothes and purse. I haven't anything."

"How'd you get the room?"

"My neighbor loaned me two hundred dollars. I paid cash for the room." She smiled a little. "At the desk they probably thought I was a hooker."

"Hookers wear makeup," I said. "Stay away from your place. Stay away from Talent."

She didn't understand. It was time that she did.

"Order us some whiskey and some cold sandwiches," I said and stood up and went in the bathroom and emptied the ice cubes in the towel into the sink. The eye looked a little better and felt a little better, and I had to concentrate on thinking, not on first aid.

When the drinks and sandwiches came, we both sat at the table and I talked, about her brother and her husband.

"Organized crime in this city has been run for years by a man named Manuel Diaz. Big Manny they call him, though he's only about five-five in thick-soled shoes. Manny's old, and he's dying. He may be dead by now."

Since escaping from Alvera, I had had time to think it through. Not all at once, but a little at a time. In cabs, at breakfast. Thoughts and recollections dodged in and out of my mind until a picture formed there. The picture had holes in it, but the pieces I saw all fit.

"What does this have to do with Norman?"

"Norm found out that the Diaz organization was laundering money. Elinor Garcia found out about the money laundering from Norm. She was killed because she learned too much about it."

"And Norman?"

"It must have looked to him as though he'd have to take the rap for killing her. Or he was afraid he'd be blamed for being her partner and wind up as dead as she did." I paused, thinking back to the night Norm had come to me in desperation. "He told me he had not gone into his apartment that night. Now I'll bet he did, and when he found Elinor Garcia's body he knew why she had been killed."

152

She shook her head. "He surely must have realized that running away was not the answer. The police would have arrested him eventually, when he returned to Tampa."

"He didn't plan on coming back to Tampa, Margaret. When he said goodbye to me in Ocala, he meant goodbye."

"Like he knew he would be killed?"

"Yes." A long silence followed my reply.

She stood up and went to the window and looked out. The light outlined her, full breasts stretching her sweater. I looked into my glass and swirled its contents. I sipped at the whiskey. The sandwiches lay untouched on their plates.

She turned and faced me and said, from where she stood, "I have to know, Paul. How did Norm learn about that underworld connection?"

"From your husband."

She closed her eyes. A jetliner reaching for altitude passed overhead, its throttles open, the roar of its engines muted by the soundproofing of the hotel. I went on. "Talent does the accounting for a man named Ray Diggs, who ostensibly owned several laundromats involved in the scheme. Talent told me about it last night. I guess he thought I would find out anyway, but if he told me he could play the role of innocent bystander. It didn't work then, and it doesn't work now. Cleaning up the money passing through four laundromats wouldn't do it for Diaz's total take. He'd need a lot more businesses to funnel cash through. He'd also need a respectable accountant as the cover, someone to arrange for bank accounts, taxes, all of it."

She stared at me. She walked slowly back to the table and sat down and picked up her drink and downed half of it. "My husband," she began, looking me in the eye, "is the accountant. He works for these gangsters."

"Yes. That's the setup. He handles not only Diggs but a number of other small businesses." I paused. "Ray Diggs wanted to see me last night. To talk, he said. He'd known Manny Diaz a long time. I think he knew something. When

153

I arrived, he was dead. Someone got to him first, someone who was afraid of what he might tell me. I suppose anyone could have done it, but the most likely candidates are Tommy Alvera and Detective Shaeffer"—I paused for an instant— "and your husband."

The color drained from her face. "No," she breathed.

I went on. "All three of them knew or could have known that Diggs was going to talk. I told Shaeffer myself. Diggs might have told your husband; they had talked just before Diggs called me. Alvera knew that I was looking for Diggs, and his men were waiting for me outside of Diggs's hotel when I left."

"Not Harold," she said. "Not that. Why, for God's sake?"

She was taking it hard. I might have know she would. He was, after all, the father of her two children. It would hurt, but she needed to know as much of it as I could tell her.

I said, "Diggs went way back with the mob. If I knew what he knew, I could say who killed him, but I don't. I can only guess. In Talent's case, it could have had something to do with the money laundering and his connection to it. He didn't want me investigating Norm and Elinor Garcia because he was afraid I would uncover the money-laundering scheme. That's why he put the squeeze on Shaeffer to get me off the case."

"But you already knew that. What could he have gained by killing that man? And what about these other men?"

"You're right, Margaret. I did already know. I also know about Shaeffer, who might have worried that Diggs knew about those payoffs. And maybe he knew about some payoffs that weren't so old. It's not what I know that got Diggs killed, it's what I don't know."

I stood up and went to the bathroom and chased two more Tylenols down with some water and returned to the bedroom and took the taste of water out of my mouth by drinking some whiskey.

She looked up at me. "And Norman? He worked with

Harold. I thought he was only doing odd jobs, trying to work off his debt. Was he working for those gangsters too?"

"I don't know," I replied and sat down, heavily, wearily. "There's something wrong there. I can feel it, but I can't come to grips with it. Like smoke, you can see it and smell it, but you can't get hold of it."

She asked, "What is it, Paul? What's wrong?"

"Me, I suppose. You see, Margaret, no one could have known where to find Norm. He didn't know himself that he would go to Jacksonville. His only plan was to take the first bus north out of Ocala. The only person who should have known that Norm was in Jacksonville was Norm."

She said, "I knew, from the postmark on his letter."

I said, "Sure, and your husband could have known too. But the letter was mailed on the day he disappeared from the barbershop. You didn't receive it until two days later."

I took a deep breath and let it out and stared for a moment toward the window, into space. My chest hurt, but it wasn't the sharp pain of a broken rib. Only bruises there. Alvera had given his boys orders not to kill me. Not then, anyway. Things had changed since then.

I looked up and saw her eyes on me, unwavering eyes that told me she remembered the desire we had once felt between us. It was there for a moment in the look she gave me and then it fled, chased by concern, by fear for me.

"What are you going to do?"

I saw no point in telling her that Alvera wanted me dead, too, before I talked too much about Garcia and Diggs and the money-laundering operation. Alvera would like to do the job himself. It was a good chance for him to settle an old score.

So I said only, "I'm working on what I'm going to do. I have the beginnings of an idea."

"What can I do to help?"

"Nothing. The only person you can do anything for is you."

She nodded. "I'll go back to the house and pack and leave

155

a note and—"

I interrupted. "First, call your neighbor and have her make sure no one is home. Then go back and get your purse, cash, checks, and credit cards. Forget hanging around to pack."

She stared at me. "It's my home. I can't leave like that."

"Listen to me, Margaret. Your husband is in a game with high stakes. It's a game for men with guns and no compunction about using them. You could get caught in the middle. You can buy clothes or anything else. Just get in and get out and go away."

She nodded her understanding and, I hoped, her agreement.

"I've called a divorce lawyer," she said. "I plan to pick up the children in Venice and drive farther south, to Fort Myers or Naples or the Keys, maybe, until the court date is set."

"That sounds good," I said. "By then everything should be cleared up."

"Yes." She looked away and stood up and went to the window. She didn't speak for several moments. She turned. She said, at last, "I don't plan to come back."

"I understand."

She returned to the chair across from me and sat down and clasped her hands together on the table. "I thought I had it all," she said. "Just what I had always wanted. Children. Home. Friends. Peace." She looked up. "No fear."

"And no commitment? When there is no fear, there's usually no commitment. That way there's nothing to be afraid of."

A faint smile came to her lips. "Maybe. About two years ago, I began to suspect that there were other women. It didn't really bother me. Well, maybe a little at first, but I adjusted. It was just the way Harold is."

"How is that, Margaret? What does Harold Talent want?"

She stared at me for a moment and then off into the distance. She looked back to me and said, "More. Always more."

156

"Until?"

"With Harold," she said, her face solemn, "there is no until. He just wants more." She paused and stared at her hands. "More of everything."

More of everything. Reason enough to become involved with the mob, I supposed. Heavy seconds passed in silence.

"Including you," I said. "I guess that's what Shaeffer meant. He has to keep you, and somehow he got the idea that he was in danger of losing his prize possession."

Her glance, defiant, jerked quickly to meet mine. "He had no reason." She paused, reflecting, eyes seeking out a spot in the air. "Maybe he did. Like you said, I was never fully committed to Harold. I suppose he sensed that." She paused again. "I don't care. Dammit, I don't care. Screw commitment."

She looked back at me. "I had that with you," she replied. "Three years of it. Three years of wondering every time you walked out the door if I'd see you alive again. Three years of fear every time I heard a siren."

"There were good times."

"Oh, yes," she said, uttering a short laugh. "Oh, God, yes. The utter joy of just having you alive and being in your arms and—" She stopped abruptly. "That's why there was Harold." She stood up and went to the window and stared out. "And he knew it, of course. He knew he'd never have all of me because part of me was still back in those three years. Part of me still belonged to you."

I got out of the chair and crossed the room and stood behind her and spoke to the back of her head. "Listen, a person's life is made up of bits and pieces from the past. Some of those pieces don't fit as neatly as we'd like, and some of them have rough edges that keep reminding us of the good and the bad. We can't do anything about that. You and I cared about each other a long time ago, and we probably still do, in ways neither of us can completely understand. We are who we are, and we have to accept that. We can't ever be what other people want us to be. We can't even be what we expect ourselves to be."

She turned to face me. "What do I want, Paul? What is it?"

"What we all want. A little bit of everything."

And then I took her into my arms and she clung to me, her arms around my neck, and we kissed, frantically, as though to make up in a few seconds for the years apart. We undressed. She paused once, for the briefest of instants, to give me a sidelong glance along her shoulder. She stood nearly naked, in silhouette, her breasts firm, nipples erect, looking at me to assure herself of something. I didn't know what. And then she went to the bed, and I followed, and she lay beneath me, her eyes closing as I began the sweet inward slide. She achieved almost instant release, and then rose again to that low-moaning, body-shuddering ecstasy.

We rested, our bodies side by side. She caressed my bruises, I caressed her delicious softness. Passion returned again, and again, and each time as it heightened, claiming us entirely, we breathed words of love to each other. Later, spent by the intensity of our joining, we slept in each other's arms.

When we awoke, the passion was gone, and only the tenderness remained. I held her and kissed her. We dressed. She sat on the end of the bed. I sat on one of the chairs at the table.

She looked across the room at me. "What I said, then, while we were making love . . ."

"It's what one says, sometimes, in that situation."

"Yes. Do you say it often?"

I gave her a steady look and an honest answer. "No."

"Me either," she said. She breathed in and out deeply. "I wish to hell I could live with you."

"We tried that once," I reminded her.

"Yes," she replied. "And we haven't changed, have we?

158

Either of us."

"Older and smarter, maybe."

"Smart enough to know it still wouldn't work?"

"Probably."

She nodded. "That's what I think too." She paused. "I still meant it, what I said about loving you. I think I needed to say it, to get it said out loud, so I couldn't keep on trying to deny it to myself any longer. I suppose the only time I could admit to feeling that way was while you made love to me."

I walked over to her and pulled her to her feet and held her by the arms and said, "I couldn't ever forget you, not in two lifetimes. Maybe not having you will be easier now, and maybe it won't. But I think it will, because we were together just now and told each other how we felt and didn't leave all the anger and hurt and need hanging for ten more years."

She nodded, her face uplifted to mine.

I kissed her, softly, and when the kiss ended I said, "Goodbye, Margaret." I walked toward the door.

She said, "Paul . . . ." I turned. "What are you going to do?"

"Three people hold cards in this game," I said. "Shaeffer, Alvera, and your husband. If I'm lucky, maybe I can play them off against each other."

"And if you're unlucky?"

I shrugged. The question needed no answer, and I don't think she expected one. You could see it was hard for her, all the old fears coming back as I headed out. She bit her lip and took a deep breath and tried to smile a little and said the words from years before. "Don't try to take on the world, hear?"

"Yeah," I said, "I hear." And then, more gently, I added, "It'll be okay, Margaret."

And I hoped my promise would not become the first lie she had ever heard from me.

13

I took a cab from the airport to where I had left my car the night before. It was parked at the curb of a quiet residential street in the Hyde Park area, not far from the minarets of the University of Tampa. It could have proved risky going back for the car, so I gave the street a careful look before leaving the cab. It was just a precaution. It was a hundred to one against either Alvera or the cops just happening across that particular vehicle, and they had not done so.

It was more dangerous out on the highway. The police would have a lookout on my license plate, and license plates are a lot easier to identify than faces. The bridges were the key points. One cop in a cruiser at each bridge could watch all the cars heading across the bay for St. Petersburg and the beaches. So I took the long way around to St. Petersburg, back streets to Oldsmar, across to Route 19, and south from there. I continued south on 34th Street past Central Avenue until I found a gas station with a pay telephone. From it, I called Shaeffer. I had decided how I was going to play both ends against the middle.

When he finally came on, I said, "I'm calling from a gas station in St. Pete. I want a private number for you, and I want you to be at that number in fifteen minutes. I have a proposition I think you'll like."

He started to give me some nonsense about not doing deals with killers, but he gave me the number anyway.

I said, "And don't bother tracing the next call. If you do, and send the St. Pete cops to collect me, you lose your chance."

"What chance?" he wanted to know.

"Don't you want to stick around and find out?" I said. I hung up and went to my car and headed it out Lakeview Avenue toward Gulfport. At 49th Street I stopped at a supermarket and found a phone and called the number he had given me. He answered, and I wasted no time on preliminaries.

"I didn't kill Ray Diggs, and you know I didn't."

"What I know, Broder, is that you were in the Imperial Palm Hotel last night about the time somebody shot him. You took a room under a phony name. You stayed about half an hour, maybe forty-five minutes, and then you left. You carry a thirty-eight, and that's what did the job. You're in real trouble, Broder."

"Someone else got there before I did," I replied. "When I went to Diggs's room, the door was open slightly. I went in. He was on the floor. I'd say he bled to death from his wounds, based on the size of the puddle around him. That had to take a little while, at least. The only way for you to make me fit the shoe is if you take the latest possible time for death to have occurred."

"Whatever it takes," he said. "There's more, you know, like his girlfriend, who says you forced your way into her apartment looking for Diggs. She's sure you killed him."

"So sure of it you could get her to testify to it?"

"Just about," he replied. "Like how you said that you would kill the sonofabitch when you caught up to him."

"She said that, huh? Did she happen to mention why I had such hard feelings toward her boyfriend?"

"She couldn't understand it," Shaeffer offered. "She was afraid of you herself, waving your gun at her and all of that sort of thing."

"Did she make all that up or did she have help in the way you asked the questions?"

"She's sure you killed her boyfriend, Broder."

I said, "But you know better. I didn't want Diggs dead. I

161

wanted him alive and singing like a canary. And you know that."

"Then who did kill him?"

"My money's on Alvera's boy," I said. "Your buddy, Max. He was standing across the street from the Imperial Palm when I left there last night. He invited me to spend the night in Alvera's guest accommodations, which I did. While I was there, I got the idea that Manny Diaz wasn't expected to last the night."

"He didn't. He died this morning, around daylight."

"Who's the heir?"

"Al Connor, according to our informant."

"How did Alvera take that?"

"Not good. I've known Tommy Alvera a long time. He's never played with a full deck. You can't reason with him. And you can't deal with him. Al Connor is a dead man."

"Maybe they'll shoot each other," I said, but my mind was on how Alvera's ambition affected me, not Connor. I hoped that Tommy was thinking about how to get rid of Connor and forgetting me in the process. On the other hand, he could figure that he could use me and what I knew about the money laundering against Connor in ways only Tommy Alvera could come up with. In any event, I'd have to deal with Alvera later. Right now, I had to get Shaeffer off my case.

While I was thinking those thoughts, Shaeffer was asking me a question in a hard voice. "You said you had a proposition. What proposition?"

"I know how I can get Talent to leave you alone, and if I do that, I want you to leave me alone."

"Leaving you alone means dropping the charges against you for the Diggs killing?"

"That's right. I need a free hand, for twenty-four hours."

"How about I arrange a limo to take you to the airport, and a first-class ticket to Brazil too?" he asked.

I ignored the sarcasm in his voice. "I can get something on Talent, Shaeffer. You wondered where he got the stuff on you. Well, I know where. I can establish his own tie to Diaz."

Silence from the other end of the line. Then, "I can't talk about that here. We'll have to meet."

"No," I said. "No cozy little meetings that'll give you a chance to shoot an armed and dangerous fugitive from a murder charge. My way or nothing. Twenty-four hours, Shaeffer. Call off the manhunt. Either that or I come in with my lawyer and a half-dozen reporters and shoot off my mouth about everything, including how Talent has the goods on you for taking payoffs."

A longer silence on the line. I gave him ten seconds. That was all I could afford. He could have a trace on the call. The cops could already be on their way, though I was counting on Shaeffer's not wanting that anymore than I did. He wanted me to himself, and he wanted me dead.

I said, "Get this, Shaeffer. I can offer you a better deal than you'll get by killing me. If you kill me, you'll get me off your back, sure. But you'll still have Talent and what he knows about you to worry about the rest of your life. If you do it my way, you'll get documents to prove Talent's own connection to the mob, stuff you can keep for the rest of your life. Talent would never dare put you on the spot again."

"What documents?"

"Uh-uh," I said. "If you knew, you might try to cut your own deal with Talent. Like trading my life to get something on him. No thanks."

"What do you get out of it?"

"You off my back, for one thing," I said. "Are you in or out, Shaeffer?"

Silence while he thought it over. "What do you want?"

"You call everybody in," I said. "Everybody, including the Pinellas County people."

"There'll be questions," he complained.

"There are always questions. Tell them you're setting a trap. Tell them anything, but give me twenty-four hours."

He thought it over. "Twelve."

163

I'd have settled for six. "All right, twelve."

"If it doesn't work, Broder, go away," he said. "Go far away. I don't want to have to kill you."

I pointed the Chevy toward Pass-a-Grille after that cheery advice. The island is narrow and long, with streets running down both sides and cross streets connecting the two long streets. The street on the Gulf side is called Gulf Way and runs parallel to the beach. I went there and parked at the end of the beach farthest from the cross street where I lived. I used the binoculars out of the Chevy's trunk to scan the length of Gulf Way. He, meaning a Pinellas County sheriff's deputy, was sitting in his cruiser just about where my street connected with Gulf Way. I put the binoculars back in the trunk and got in and drove away from there, heading north. When I passed Don-Ce-Sar and saw no official car in my rearview mirror, I breathed out a lot of trapped air. I had not realized I was so tense.

I drove up the beaches as far as Madeira Beach, thinking that Shaeffer would need time to explain to his superiors why he was pulling everyone in. He'd also need time to get it done.

I parked at a restaurant. Next to the restaurant was a small motel. I sat and watched the traffic go by from the restaurant's parking lot. No sheriff's deputies passed.

I went inside the restaurant and got a double whiskey at the bar. The bartender put it in a plastic cup at my request, and I went outside and crossed the parking lot and a narrow grassy strip to the motel. I needed a phone and a private place to talk. Using an outside pay phone had been essential for my conversation with Shaeffer. He could have traced my call. Harold Talent could not.

I rented a room and went to it and added a little water to the whiskey and sat on the edge of the bed and called Harold Talent's office. His secretary put him on the phone. He

164

wanted to know what I wanted. He didn't sound friendly.

"Your client," I said, "bought the farm last night." I had to explain. "Ray Diggs. He called me. Did a lot of talking. Wanted to do some more, in person, but a gun put a stop to that sort of nonsense."

"I see. What does that have to do with me?"

"Diggs was, and you are, in business with people who take a dim view of talking to outsiders. Guys like Tommy Alvera."

He tried to bluff. "I've no idea what you're talking about."

"You're up to your ass with the mob," I said, "helping them to clean up their dirty money. According to Tommy Alvera, with whose boys I spent most of last night, it was Al Connor's idea. People that he and Manny Diaz could trust found themselves set up in various small businesses, not too lucrative but all dealing in cash. More cash came from illegal activities—drug deals, prostitution, gambling, you name it—and started flowing through these businesses."

He tried changing the subject. "Have you seen my wife, Broder? I'm worried about her."

"Sure," I said and went on. "But to really dress it up and make it look legitimate, the mob needed a first-class accountant, respectable but poor and not liking it. They needed someone like you, because sloppy bookkeeping could lead to problems with the IRS and maybe then the FBI and who knows who else. They also needed someone they could trust because the people who ostensibly owned the businesses weren't supposed to touch the dirty money that was passing through."

"You're guessing, Broder."

"Some of it, yes," I admitted. "I'm guessing it started small and grew as you earned Manny Diaz's trust. His boys turned over the cash to you, and your bookkeeping tricks did the rest. You probably set up phony suppliers you could write checks to, for example. As the operation grew, you got Norm to come in with you, cashing checks and making deposits. Those are pretty good guesses, aren't they?"

165

"What's the purpose of this call?" he asked.

"To save my life."

"Totally immaterial to me."

"I don't doubt it," I replied. "But you're going to help, or you're going to lose your ass."

"You don't worry me, Broder."

"Try this. Suppose I go to the feds, maybe the FBI or the IRS, and lay it all out for them. You don't think they'd be interested?"

He thought it over. "I don't think you would do that. You would then become the sole witness. That's a tempting motive for certain people to want to remove you permanently."

"The government would protect me."

"Not forever."

"Long enough to send you to jail."

"Afterward, you'd die," Talent said, his voice flat, without emotion. "I would be in prison only a few years. You'd be dead forever. Not a good bargain for you."

"For neither of us. I have a better one."

"I can't wait to hear it."

"It goes like this," I said. "You bring me the Diggs account books for the last two years, the real ones and the ones you have ready for the tax people. I also want you to bring his check registers and his income tax returns. To that you add the same stuff from at least one other business that is a front for the organization. You pick whichever one you want."

"How generous of you."

"You also make three copies of all that stuff, one of which you get to keep. You bring me the originals and two copies."

"Why would I do that?" he asked.

"Because you don't want to go to jail. If you do it my way, everybody wins. Nobody goes to jail, nobody dies."

His silence indicated that he was thinking it through. He said, after a few seconds, "What do you intend to do with all that material?"

"One copy goes to Shaeffer, for his personal protection.

166

If he has that stuff on you, you can't lean on him any longer, and he'll stop leaning on me." I paused. "The originals I keep, as insurance. They go into a safe place, for reading only in case of my death, say before the age of ninety. That way, your pals have no incentive to kill me, unless I make them mad by shooting off my mouth to the cops, which I don't plan to do."

"I see. All very neat." Talent paused. His orderly mind probably noted one omission. "And the second copy?"

"That goes to Al Connor, to prove I can deliver the originals, just in case anybody gets the idea I'm bluffing."

He didn't like it and told me so. "He'll know the material came from me."

"Sure, and he'll probably get a new bookkeeper," I said. "But as long as everybody stays cool, the money laundering can continue. That's what Connor will want. You won't get a gold watch for your efforts, but Connor has no percentage in killing you and drawing attention to what you've been doing for him. You may have to go straight, but you ought to do that anyway."

"I'll think about your proposal. Where can I call you?"

"You can't," I said. "And there is no time for you to think about it. You just start copying. It'll take a while for you to collect everything and copy it." I looked at my watch. "I'll call again in two hours and tell you where to bring the stuff."

He wanted to argue, to quibble. I told him I had no time for splitting hairs. He'd have the stuff ready for delivery to me in two hours, or I would go to the FBI. He agreed, then, but he wasn't finished. He had one other thing on his mind.

"Where is she, Broder? There with you? That's what she wants. That's what she's always wanted."

"What she wanted, Talent, was what she thought you represented: solid, middle-class respectability. An ordered, assured life, where tomorrow would be like today, and next year the same as this year only maybe a little better. A nice suburb where everybody cuts their grass on Saturdays and you take your kids to orthodontists and play tennis or golf at the club. A place away from the dirt and grime and grit of life, away from the violence, away from the fear. A lot of people want that, Talent, and it's not a bad thing to want." I paused, feeling the anger building up in me, knowing that giving way to those feelings would do no one any good. I said, "Two hours, Talent, and you'd better hope I don't change my mind."

I slept for an hour and a half and woke up groggily to the ringing of the phone beside the bed. A man's voice reminded me that I had asked to be awakened.

I thanked the voice and went to the bathroom and splashed cold water on my face. I looked it over. My cheeks were red, hot, and flushed-looking. The eye that had been closed was now open but surrounded by a purple and black bruise, going yellowish around the sides.

Each time I moved, I felt new places that hurt. I took some Tylenol and wished for whiskey to wash it down but knew that too much whiskey would slow my reaction time.

I returned to the bedroom and used the telephone to check my answering service. The only message to interest me was one from Margaret at the airport hotel.

I called her. "You okay?" I asked.

She said she was. "I did what you suggested. I went home and retrieved my purse and left immediately." She paused. "Paul . . ." She hesitated, unsure of whether to continue. I prompted her, and she said, "Is it possible that someone could be watching our house?"

Caution signals blipped across the horizon of my mind. "What gave you that idea?"

"We live on a cul-de-sac. At the corner where I turn in, this car was parked. You know how you just automatically come to know all the cars in your neighborhood? Well, I'd never seen this one before."

"Could be anything," I said. "Someone waiting for one of your neighbors to arrive home. Maybe someone on your

168

block has fallen behind in their car payments, and the repo man is out there." I paused, keeping my voice casual. "What kind of car?"

"I don't know what make, but it was green and had those dark windows you can't see through. I thought someone was in the car, but I couldn't be sure. By the time I got my things and left again, the car was gone."

I assured her it probably meant nothing, and my assurance seemed to work. When we hung up, her voice sounded relaxed.

I thought about the car Margaret had described. It was not the car that Tony and Max had used to take me to see Alvera. Of course, Alvera would have other men to call upon for grunt work like stakeouts.

I shrugged off the idea that Alvera was involved and told myself what I had told her, that it could be anything.

I walked back to the restaurant parking lot and retrieved the Chevy and drove it back to Pass-a-Grille.

I saw only one official car and that was a St. Pete Beach cruiser. The sole cop inside was looking for speeders. The sheriff's cruiser had left its station at the end of my street. I took that as confirmation that Shaeffer had kept his end of our deal. He couldn't afford not to.

Before turning into the alley, I drove around the streets adjacent to my place, twice, to be sure. After that, I entered the alley, driving slowly, tires crunching on the crushed shells, the sound loud in the still evening. Everything looked quiet, peaceful, unthreatening.

I had given a lot of thought to the best place to meet Talent and had settled on the motel from where I had called him. Now I had a better idea. Why not where I would be most comfortable? Why not the place where I lived?

I had to go inside anyway. The .45 automatic was in there, in the ceiling above the closet. Alvera's boys had taken my .38 revolver, the piece I usually carry, and I had no chance

169

to get it back. The .45 was all I had left. I was beginning to feel vulnerable walking around without a gun, especially since all my current and potential enemies seemed to have guns, including whoever had gotten to Ray Diggs before me.

I parked the car two blocks away, in front of a vacant cottage, and walked back to my place. I went in and retrieved the gun and asked myself that question again. Why not here? The answer came back in the affirmative. The cops had left, and if Alvera thought there was any chance I'd have returned home after escaping, his boys would have checked the house hours ago and would not return.

I called Talent. He was irritable, having had to wait well past the two hours I had set for my call. He wanted me to come to his office, but I told him no thanks and gave him directions to the place at Pass-a-Grille.

After that, I started the coffee maker and grilled a hamburger, in the dark, and ate it. I had no holster for the .45, so I stuck it in my belt and walked around the house closing all the draperies. When that was finished, I went into the living room and turned on the two table lamps and sat down with a mug of hot coffee to wait for a man who hated me.

Talent arrived a little after nine. He had brought me a stack of stuff, six account books on top of the pile, two cardboard cartons under that, and a much thicker ledger on the bottom under it all. He carried the pile in both hands. It looked heavy, all that paper.

I took out my gun and pointed it at him and turned on the ceiling light in the dining ell. "On the table," I said.

He looked at the gun and marched to the table, breathing heavily, with his load. He put his stack down on the end near the kitchen and stood by the table, one hand on the topmost ledger. He took several deep breaths and looked at the gun again and then at my eyes.

"Do you also want my wallet and car keys?" he sneered.

"Turn around," I said. "Against the wall, legs spread." He

170

did it like he'd had practice. The more I got to know Harold Talent, the more likely I thought it was that he had some experience along those lines in Chicago.

I patted him down and took away a little .25 automatic. I dropped his gun into my jacket pocket and stuck my gun in my belt and went to the other end of the table and sat down. "Let's see what you have, now that we're all friendly." He sat down and looked balefully across the short table. He pushed the top account book to me without uttering a word. On the cover it said SUNSHINE COIN-O-MATIC.

I opened the book and saw computer-printed sheets. I lifted my eyes to his and said, "It's not in your handwriting."

"Welcome to the twentieth century, Broder."

I ignored his sarcasm. "If you have a pen with you, get it out and start signing some of these pages. Just the originals."

His hesitation lasted only a moment. He took from the inside of his jacket a gold-plated Cross pen and began signing. After ten minutes or so, he had gone through the top ledgers, and then he laid the pen aside and wiggled his fingers to work out the cramps.

I pulled the books to me and looked at what he had signed.

"Satisfied?" he asked.

"And the photocopies?"

"In the boxes." He tapped one forefinger against the cartons which came next in the pile.

"Then I'm satisfied," I said. "Or I will be, after we go through these and you point out how you worked the phony businesses." I nodded toward the final ledger, the thick one on the bottom of the pile. "What's in that one?"

He pushed aside the boxes and lifted the cover and put his hand inside the ledger. "This," he said and showed me the business end of .38 snubby. "Hands on the table, Broder."

I did what he ordered, all too conscious of the .45 stuck uselessly inside the waistband of my trousers. He had suckered me, and I didn't know why.

Unless, of course, he intended to kill me.

171

14

"STAND UP," HE ordered. "Very carefully." I did. "Take off your jacket," he said. "Now the gun in your belt. Move slowly, Broder. Jacket on the table. Gun on top of it."

When he had things the way he wanted them, he fished into my jacket for his .25 and dropped it into his own jacket pocket and laid my .45 on the floor and kicked it to the side. I watched it go spinning off through the doorway into the darkened bedroom.

He backed up a few steps and waved the barrel of his revolver in my direction. "Over there," he said. "On the couch. You will sit on your hands."

The couch sat against the wall opposite the front door, a blond wood end table at one end, between the couch and one of the room's two chairs. The tall brass lamp on the table helped illuminate the room.

I went and put my hands behind me and sat on them. The brown and orange and green print fabric beneath my hands felt surprisingly rough.

I looked up at him. "What's the point?" I asked him. "We had a deal where nobody gets hurt. All you lose is your hold over Shaeffer and your job with the organization. It's not worth risking a murder rap."

"Only if I get caught," he replied, smiling, "do I need to worry about that."

"This is a very quiet little town, Talent. Guns make a lot of noise. You'll be lucky to get off the island, and if you do there will be witnesses to your leaving."

He almost smiled. "It's a cool night. Most people have

their windows closed."

"Not mine. I like the fresh air."

The almost smile stayed on his face. "Other people's windows, then. Other people watching television. And I won't run to my car and appear to flee. It's only a few steps. I can be on my way in seconds."

"It's still a risky proposition. Especially," I lied, "with Shaeffer outside watching the house to make sure that his interests are protected."

The smile faded, and his face showed a moment of fear. You could see in his eyes that the mind behind the eyes was busy calculating the possibilities.

"No," he said at last. "You would not bring Shaeffer in on this. Too much risk of him taking all the material and leaving you out in the cold. Or dead." He smiled coldly. "You had all the bases covered. All but one."

"Which one was that?" My eyes measured the distance between us as I asked the question. He stood halfway to the front door. That made it about seven or eight feet from me, sitting, to him standing. The chance of me jumping him was slim, but slim is better than none. But, even for slim, I needed an opening, a fraction of a second of inattention.

"That I'm more intelligent than you."

"Not so much that you could keep your wife from walking out on you." Keep him talking; keep hoping for an opening.

His eyes grew hot. "Where is she?" he demanded. He raised the gun, aiming for my chest.

"I can't tell you if I'm dead," I told him. "But I will if you let me walk out of here."

Some of the fire in his eyes faded. "No. You stay. You will die, and after you're dead she'll come back to me. She belongs to me, Broder. She'll come back when you are no longer around to lure her away from me."

"She doesn't belong to anyone. Your gears are loose if you think that killing me will get her back."

He cackled. "Beg, Broder, beg for your life. I wish she could be here to see it."

I'm not against begging, certainly not when the situation calls for it. I just didn't see how it would help me then. My performing for Talent would only concentrate his attention on me. What I needed was to direct his attention elsewhere. Like on his prized possessions, his books.

I nodded toward the dinette table. "How do you figure to get out of here in mere seconds," I said, "when you have to gather up all that stuff and lug it out of here?"

His eyes stayed on mine. "I'll manage." He hesitated as if he wanted to tell me something before he pulled the trigger. "I think I always feared you would try to come back into her life. When that fool of a brother insisted on involving you—" He stopped abruptly and raised the gun a little.

I talked fast. "All that Margaret wanted from me was to clear her brother of a murder charge. You made it more."

His glance met mine. More. Something more. I saw it in his eyes and realized he needed to know what I might have only guessed at. What I could guess, others could also guess. That's what worried him. That's what he had to know before he disposed of me.

He asked, "What more, Broder?"

My memory went full circle, from the night Norm Colquist sat in that same room until the present, with Talent pointing a gun at me, ready to be rid of me once and for all. What more?

It did not come to me with a sudden flash of insight. I had to work through it from the beginning. Jealousy? More than that. The jealousy was genuine, but he was using it as a cover for something he wanted to keep hidden. Since it was genuine, it made a good cover. A cover for what? Something more. Something he was ready to kill me for. Something I knew, or something I could find out. That he worked for the mob?

No. He knew I wasn't planning to make a noise about the

174

money-laundering scheme. I would not risk a plastic bag over my head and a truck wheel tied to my ankles for nothing. The deal I had offered him was simple, straightforward. And it depended upon me keeping my mouth shut.

I would keep my mouth shut, super shut. Like Elinor Garcia? She learned all there was to learn, but she kept her mouth shut. She had told no one. Or had she?

That was getting me nowhere. What did I know, or what did Talent think I knew, that made me dangerous? Nothing that I could see. Nothing. I only knew he ran the money-laundering scheme, and the only people I planned to tell were Shaeffer, who couldn't do anything about it, and Al Connor, who already knew about it.

It couldn't be me, then, or what I knew. More. Something more. If it wasn't what I knew, it had to be something I planned to do. The hell of it was, I didn't plan to do anything except forget. I planned to forget Talent and Garcia and Diggs and Norm and all the rest, just as soon as I had my insurance and delivered the copies of Talent's books.

Talent's voice hissed at me. "What more, Broder?"

The books. It wasn't me, it was the books, but I had to die, because if he refused me the books I'd go to the Feds and that would be just as bad. So it was something in his ledgers that he feared. Who cared? I didn't; the ledgers were just insurance. Shaeffer? No. To him, the same. That left only Al Connor to find something in Talent's books, something that Talent would kill to prevent Connor from knowing.

The answer nearly took my breath away. It was so simple, yet so unbelievable. Talent didn't seem the type, didn't seem to have the bare-balled nerve to pull it off. Wanting more, always more, may have blinded him to the danger in the beginning. Once started, it was too late to turn back.

I let out a deep breath. "You've been skimming," I said. "You've been stealing from Manny Diaz. From the mob. It's in the books, isn't it? Your accounts will show payments to phony companies that the organization doesn't know anything about. That's a death sentence, if they ever find out."

"That's why you have to die, Broder. I can't let you send those books to Connor. If he or Tommy Alvera ever found —"

The door behind Talent pushed open and a new voice said, "If I ever found what, Harold?"

Talent began turning.

Alvera said, "Put the gun down, Harold." Alvera stood to the side of the doorway. He had his left hand in his jacket pocket. His right hand held a gun, an automatic with a silencer screwed to its snout. Beside him stood Max, a similar gun in each hand. I saw no sign of Tony.

Max pocketed one of his guns and stepped forward and took Talent's gun and pushed him in the chest toward one of the living room chairs. Talent dropped backward into it, his face ashen.

Alvera pulled up the other chair and sat down in it, balancing his gun on his knee. He said to Max, "Look around."

It took only a moment. It was a small house. Max returned and reported. "It's okay." He leaned against the wall, watching.

Alvera grunted. He looked at me. "Tough guy, huh? Let a fucking accountant get the drop on you." His eyes swept the room, taking in the ledgers on the table. "Doing your homework?"

Talent spoke up quickly. "He forced me to show him the books on the company's money operation. He planned to go to the police with it all, if he wasn't cut in."

"Yeah?" replied Alvera. "How'd he force you? The guy that followed you here didn't say anything about that. He said you came out of your office with an armload of account books and got in your car and drove over here like you were going to a board meeting."

Talent wet his lips with his tongue. "He said that . . . that he'd hunt me down and kill me if I didn't do what he said."

Alvera turned his blank stare to me. "You say that,

176

Broder? You threaten one of Manny's good friends?" I stared back, saying nothing. "You're going to die soon, Broder. After Mr. Talent and I get a few things straightened out."

He turned his glance back to Talent. "You should have called me, Harold. I could have taken care of you."

"Yes," replied Talent, his voice thick. "Yes. That was a mistake on my part. I wasn't thinking clearly."

"The old man's dying probably upset you."

"Yes. Yes, it did. It really did. I thought a lot of Mr. Diaz. He was like a second father to us all."

"Yeah," said Alvera. "A second father. I like that, Harold. You talk good. Smart boy, that's what Al Connor always said. Now, about how you been skimming on Al. I want to hear about that."

"That's Broder," replied Talent quickly. "He's trying to stir up trouble. That's all it is. I told him he'd be in trouble with you if he kept it up."

Alvera leaned forward, teeth bared. "You're the one in trouble, Talent, you lying sonofabitch. You been knocking down on Manny Diaz like you was a fucking street whore."

"No," pleaded Talent, hoarseness filling his voice. "It's a lie. Broder . . . Broder made it up."

"Yeah," said Alvera. "With you holding a gun on him." He leaned back against his chair. "You went to college, didn't you, Talent? Like Al Connor. Me, I quit school in tenth grade. I got my education on the street. No fucking books out on the street. Hey, Max. You know what's in books? Nothing but fucking stories." Alvera grinned. "Stories about fairies and shit. Ain't that right, Max?"

"Right," said Max, never taking his eyes from me, as though I would disappear again as I had last night.

Alvera said, "You read all that shit, and you think you're smart. Smart, sure. You're dumb as shit, Talent." He paused. "Say it."

Talent looked at me and then at the floor. "I'm dumb as

shit," he said quietly.

"Louder," ordered Alvera. "So Max can hear it. And you're a pile of shit, too."

Talent repeated it all. Max grinned. Alvera grinned. He liked his new game. He turned to me. "Your turn."

I said, "Max, get your boss to tell you about the time I took him down and took his gun away from him."

Alvera's grin faded. His scar whitened. "In a few minutes, you'll be dead, tough guy." He turned to Talent. "You want to join him?"

Talent wet his lips again. "No," he said hoarsely.

"Then you're going to write a letter for me," Alvera said. He looked around the room, stood up and put his gun inside his jacket, and went to the table and tore a page out of one of the ledgers. He took it to Talent. "Write on this. Make it to Al Connor. Tell him that you did what he wanted you to do about skimming from Mr. Diaz. Tell him that you want to give him his share and then you want out because Tommy Alvera will catch on, that Alvera ain't old and sick like Mr. Diaz was when Al cooked up the scheme to double-cross poor old Mr. Diaz."

Talent looked up at his tormentor. "It's my death warrant."

"Write it," said Alvera, "and I'll give you a chance to get out of town, save your ass."

I said, "If you believe that, Talent, you'll believe anything."

Alvera looked at me and smiled coldly. "He'll believe it if he wants to get out of here alive." He turned back to Talent. "Besides, there's Mrs. Talent."

Something inside me turned cold.

Alvera continued, "Tell him, Max."

"She's at the airport Marriott," Max said. He gave the number of the room she was in.

Alvera picked it up from there. "I wanted to know what you were up to, Harold. So I had someone watching both your house and your office. Your wife showed up at your house late this afternoon in a hell of a hurry. My man got curious and followed her. Damn good luck. I now got two men in the room across the hall from her. If I get what I want from you, I don't have to call them, and if I don't call them in the next hour or so they'll go away. If I don't get it, I call and they move in on her."

Talent looked at me, his mouth moving, no words coming. His ashen face and his wide eyes showed his fear.

"Write it," I said, "after Alvera calls off his dogs."

Alvera said, "After the letter." He took his gun from his pocket and pushed it against Talent's neck. "Last chance."

Talent said he'd write the letter. He spoke in a voice not much louder than a whisper. It was hard for me to hear him.

I said, "He's got us. He doesn't have her. And he doesn't have the letter. He's not going to kill you, not until he gets the letter. Make him let her go first, Talent, damn you. He's going to kill you and me anyway."

"No," he said. He was too far gone in fear for rational argument. He wanted to believe that Alvera would keep his word. He wanted to believe that death was banished. He looked up at Alvera, his eyes pleading. "You'll let me go, like you said?"

"Sure," said Tommy Alvera, killer. "Why the hell not?"

Talent eagerly wrote the letter and handed it to Alvera. Alvera glanced at it, handed it to Max. Max read it and said, "It's okay, Tommy. Just what you wanted." He handed the letter back to Alvera. Alvera folded it and put it inside his jacket.

Alvera said, "Stand up, Harold."

"It's okay, Tommy?" he asked in a whisper as he stood. "I did okay?"

"Yeah. You'll be okay. I promise. But I can't take any chances while I deal with Broder."

Talent assured him that he understood and turned around and put his hands behind his back when Alvera ordered it.

179

Alvera took some tough, clear plastic packing tape from his pocket and wrapped it around Talent's wrists. Talent bleated out a reminder to Alvera of Alvera's promise, and then knelt on the floor when Alvera told him to.

Talent looked up at me. His mouth was open, slack. You could see in his eyes that he knew what was coming. He was just beginning to believe it, to understand. He tried to speak, but fear constricted his vocal cords.

He opened his mouth to scream, but Alvera slapped a piece of tape over it. He had the bag out the next moment and placed it over Talent's head and wrapped the tape around his neck.

The bag was made of clear plastic, like the tape. Talent's eyes bugged out. He tried to get up. He fell. He rubbed his head against the floor, tying to rip the bag away from his face. His nostrils, sucking air, got plastic up them instead. His feet kicked the floor. His face turned a bluish tint, shiny with his death sweat. His eyes were huge frantic orbs. He rolled on the floor. The movement stopped. He made one final kick and lay still.

Alvera was grinning. Max was watching, his face impassive, probably used to the sight, if anyone could ever get used to it.

Alvera's gun was still in his pocket, as was one of Max's. Max held his other gun tightly and pointed it toward the dying man. Max's only reaction as he watched Talent do his death dance was a whitening of the knuckles on the hand that held the gun.

I moved. Not toward the two gunmen but away from them, toward the bedroom. They each had guns, and I didn't. I needed to even things up a little.

I was off the couch and halfway across the room while they still watched Talent to see if he had another movement left to him. I was in the room and had the door shut behind me when the first shots came, two of them, close together. They hit the door and made a ripping sound as they smashed the

180

thin veneer of the hollow-core door before burying themselves in the opposite wall.

The bullets made tiny holes. I saw specks of light coming through from the part of the house where Alvera and Max remained. Inside the bedroom was total darkness. And sudden quiet. Alvera wouldn't chance random firing and the possibility of bullets escaping my house and frightening the neighbors into calling the police. He or Max would shoot next only when they had me in their sights.

I found myself breathing heavily, shaking inside. The first thing was to find my gun, which I had last seen spinning across the floor into the darkness of the bedroom. I got down on my hands and knees and began seeking in the direction the gun had taken. From outside the bedroom came muffled voices, Tommy and Max discussing tactics, probably.

My crawling progress brought me to the bed. I used the full length of my right arm to sweep an arc under the bed. No gun. Inwardly I cursed; I blasphemed. I had to have that gun.

I turned and crawled toward the window and crawled into glass, cutting both hands but not severely. No gun there either. Only glass, broken glass, where I had to break out the jalousie to escape from Tony and Max on the previous night. By now they would have figured out how I had managed it. Hiding in the attic wouldn't work again.

The worst of thoughts filtered through my mind. I had no place to hide.

I heard a sound outside the broken window. Footsteps on the gravel. The clicking sound of an automatic being cocked. Now I knew where Tony was. I had no place to hide, no place to run.

My fingers groped and felt a shard of glass, eight or nine inches long. It cut me as I felt around it, sizing it up. It had a needle point at one end and razor edges along its length.

I took my handkerchief from my rear pocket and wrapped it around the widest end of the shard. They'd be coming soon.

The glass was the only weapon I had.

I sat on the floor, trying to make my mind think ahead. I had to guess what they'd do when they made their move. One of them would come through the door, not through the window. It would be too difficult to crawl through a narrow window ready to shoot.

They might worry that I had a gun. They couldn't be sure I didn't. They'd come in with guns firing, or at least one of them would. The doorway would accommodate only one at a time.

Max. It would have to be Max. That's what Alvera paid him for. Max would come, and he would come soon. Any time now.

I moved silently to the wall beside the door. I flattened my back against the wall. I held the shard of glass in my right hand, my flesh protected from the razor-sharp edges by the handkerchief. I waited. The wait lasted for only a few seconds.

I sensed movement on the other side of the door. Someone was coming. Someone stood only the thickness of the door away from me.

Max's kick, shattering the door around the knob, ended the silence in the room. The door swung open. Light streamed in around his solitary figure. He had a gun in each hand. Both guns coughed repeatedly with the softened sound of the noise suppressor at work.

I pivoted on my left foot, my right arm swinging in an arc. The shard plunged into Max's stomach. Its edges sliced through the handkerchief, cutting my right hand. I didn't stop to think what those same edges were doing to Max's belly and intestines. I twisted the shard.

He screamed and staggered one step back and then two forward. He dropped both guns to clutch at the agony in his gut. He staggered forward and fell face down on the floor. His hips pumped upward once, twice, in an obscene imitation of intercourse. After the second time, he lay still.

182

I picked up one of the guns in my right hand. It slipped a little from the bleeding where the glass had cut me. I tore a piece out of my shirt and managed to get enough of the cloth around my hand to hold the gun.

Then something hammered my left shoulder back against the wall. I saw Tony's head and shoulders leaning into the window, his arm extended in front of him. He held a gun. My mind registered the fact that he was firing the gun. Firing at me.

I squeezed the trigger of the gun in my hand, again and again and again. Tony grunted and leaned forward and seemed to rest his chest on the window sill and let his head slump against the inside wall. His arm dangled toward the floor. His gun still hung by the trigger guard from his cramped index finger. His blood traced thin dark lines down the wall from the window.

For a moment, all was silence. My left arm would not move. I felt sick, dizzy, suddenly cold.

Tommy Alvera's voice came softly from the other room. "Max? Tony?"

A shadow flicked into and out of the path of light that fell across the floor and window of the bedroom from the open door.

Alvera was looking for his men. And he had found them.

It looked like my best chance. He would be close to the door, possibly stunned by knowing that I had finished both of his men and that he was alone. I had to move fast. I pivoted once more on my left foot, slowly as in a dream, turning into the light of the doorway, the dead Max's gun in my hand, ready.

Alvera's blurred figure stood facing me, his eyes like empty black holes. He breathed heavily through his mouth. He held his gun in his right hand. Two guns, two right hands.

My own gun seemed far away from me. I squeezed the trigger and heard three sharp sounds. I felt a shock of pain in my leg above the knee.

183

The pain cleared my vision for a moment. I began to fall, twisting and squeezing the trigger again. Falling, I saw a hole from the bullet appear in the ceiling and the dust from the punctured wallboard puff out around it.

And then I was on the floor, looking up at Tommy Alvera. He pointed his gun at me and cursed me for the death of his men and screamed his hatred of me and jerked his shoulders in a manic dance of frustration that I was dying and that killing me was the worst that he could do to me and that it wasn't enough.

The pain in my leg had me fully conscious. I could see Alvera and his gun and every detail in the room clearly and knew that he would soon pull the trigger, and it would all end. But not quite yet.

Alvera calmed. He said, "Hang on for a little while, you sonofabitch." He bent close to me. "You're going out, Broder. You're fucking dying. And I'm alive." He stood up and put his left hand on his hip and waved his gun in the air and laughed hysterically, all of his fear suddenly gone. "All you other fuckers are dead, and I'm alive. Alive, you bastards. Tommy Alvera is going to live for fucking ever."

I tried to move my left leg. I felt no more pain in it, nor could I feel movement. Nothing on my left side seemed to work. I could drag myself only with my right arm, kneel on only my right leg

Alvera looked down at me once more and bared his teeth and stared and said, "You hang on, Broder, while I get my boys on the phone. You gotta hear that woman screaming as you die, you sonofabitch. Over the phone, huh, what d'ya say? She'll die hard, and you'll hear her all the way, baby."

I got off my back.

He said, "That's it, baby. Stay alive so's you can hear her screaming while they cut off her nipples."

He started backing away, toward the phone, his gun pointed at me, taking no chances.

I managed to get up on one knee, my right hand balancing me in that position. I fought dizziness and nausea and the certain knowledge that I would soon pass out.

I crawled a yard to the couch. Alvera encouraged it. He had the gun. He had nothing to fear. He said, "Even if you go to hell first, you'll know she's on her way." He kept backing toward the telephone. He had only a few steps to go before he could put out his hand and pick up the receiver and dial the hotel and instruct his men.

If I fainted or died, there was nothing I could do to prevent it. I drew air, lots of it, into my lungs and clutched at the couch and dragged myself forward.

I swayed on my one good knee. I held onto the couch with all the strength I had in my good arm, balanced precariously. If I fell, I wouldn't get up again. Somehow I knew that.

Alvera had only to step around Harold Talent's body to reach the telephone. But his eyes and his thoughts remained on me, on how he would exact his final revenge, on how he would remind me of the night that I had humiliated him. Tommy Alvera had a long memory.

But not long enough to remember the corpse behind him, the corpse of the man he had humiliated and tricked and murdered. Alvera's left foot backed into the corpse's leg. Alvera lost his balance. His arms went up, flailing, trying to regain his footing, failing. He fell backward. His hands, groping for support, lost the grip he had on his gun. He went down.

I crawled toward him, holding to anything that offered support.

He saw me and twisted to recover his gun. It lay two arm lengths away from him. He crawled toward it.

The dizziness was returning to me, and no longer could I fend it off. The room seemed to blur.

But I reached the gun first, as his fingers crabbed toward it. I had only seconds of consciousness left. After that, Alvera would make his call and Margaret would die in agony.

I had to stop him, and there was only one way. I swayed

185

and fell as I reached for the gun. I felt its weight in my hand. Alvera crawled toward me, his hands clutching for my throat. He saw that I had the gun, and his eyes widened as he stared into its barrel from a yard away.

And then, just before I passed out, I shot him three times in the face.

15

FACES PEERED IN at me. The faces changed, became older or younger, masculine or feminine. The heads stayed the same, all hairless and bulbous green. Green everywhere, green heads and green bodies and a bright light and then no light and no faces.

Dreams, lots of dreams. Margaret Talent came to me in a dream, and her lips felt cool against my forehead. And ghosts came in my dream, dead men, forgotten men, people I didn't recognize. Sometimes they stood, statuelike, voiceless; sometimes they moved; sometimes they even spoke. But their faces changed, and their bodies changed, and their voices sounded strange. Only Margaret seemed never to change.

Norm appeared in my dreams, changed like the rest and beyond my reach. I wanted him to stay, I wanted to tell him that it was not my fault, and I heard myself screaming, and a white shadow appeared on either side of me and held me, and after a while I floated on a soft white cloud.

They told me later that I had recovered consciousness on the sixth day in a St. Petersburg hospital. The next day the cops came to see me, two of them in street clothes. One was named Rodriguez; he was from Tampa and told me that there was a guard outside my door.

"To keep me in?" Hardly necessary. I was too weak to move.

Rodriguez replied, "To keep people out. Seemed like a good idea, seeing what you did to the Connor mob. All your visitors have to sign in: name, address, and identification."

187

The Connor mob. So the scepter had passed.

Rodriguez went on. "You're in the clear. Self-defense. Your gun was in the corner of the bedroom. Not a shot fired. Alvera and his boys jumped you. All you have to do is confirm it, when you're ready to give us a statement."

"What about Mrs. Talent? She okay?"

"Yeah. Why not?"

I closed my eyes again, remembering. Alvera could not make his telephone call because he was dead. I had killed him.

They went away, and the next day I talked to other police, and five days later I dictated a statement to a police stenographer. The Tampa police had gone into Talent's office and picked up Talent's books that he kept on nearly thirty businesses that fronted for the laundering of the mob's money. That kept the Tampa cops busy. The IRS, the FBI, and the U.S. Attorney for Florida's Middle District all got into the act.

As they dug into the maze of Harold Talent's inspired bookkeeping, they discovered hidden bank accounts maintained by Talent under various aliases. The money he had stolen from the Diaz organization had gone into those accounts. Talent had withdrawn twenty thousand from one of the accounts two days before Norm fled town. For the rest, nothing had been touched. It all belonged to the government now.

After three weeks I went to a convalescent home south of Tampa. The police said it was a secret move and the convalescent home admitted me under the name of Paul Shoup.

About ninety percent of the other residents were old enough to be my parents. Some were old enough to be my grandparents. I avoided all of them, keeping to my private room, venturing out to the broad terrace in my wheelchair only after sundown, when the terrace was empty and the evenings too cool for the older bones.

188

At the end of the second week, Rodriguez came to see me. He said, "We hear Al Connor is looking for you. We better move you again."

I said, "No. I can't spend my life running away from guys like Al Connor."

He shrugged. "Suit yourself." He paused. "I still have the murders of Elinor Garcia and Ray Diggs on my hands."

"Harold Talent killed them."

He shook his head. "He was in Naples when Garcia got it."

"Norm Colquist lied about calling Talent in Naples. That's why the phone company had no record of any calls that Norm made." I paused. "Talent had to kill her because she learned about his skimming from the organization. She had been sleeping with Norm and probably picked up a little here and a little there."

"Like the name of Ray Diggs," he suggested.

"Yes. She pumped Diggs, and he talked because he thought he could get her into bed. She probably asked him about the phony companies that Talent wrote checks to. Diggs began to suspect that she was on to the money-laundering operation. He didn't realize until much later that she had turned up a lot more than that. Later, after she was killed, he thought that Alvera had killed her. Diggs also feared Alvera might find out it was Diggs who talked too much, and he'd be next on Alvera's list. When he saw Alvera's men covering his hotel, he panicked and pulled out."

"All right," he said. "Garcia found out that Talent was skimming. She wanted a piece of the action. Talent does not want another partner, so he takes her out with five bullets. Diggs gets it the same way. Talent again?"

"Yes. Diggs thought he could trust Talent. He asked Talent to talk to me, to get me to leave him alone. When that didn't work, he called me directly and set up a meeting. He must have started thinking there was more to it than he had

189

originally thought. I think he began to suspect Talent, because he told me he had someone in mind to set up for having done the talking that he planned to do. I think he planned that Talent would take the fall."

"If Diggs told Talent he had a deal with you, Talent would have become suspicious. Why would Diggs tell him?"

"I don't think Diggs thought Talent was dangerous. After all, Diggs knew Talent only as a bookkeeper, and if Talent pleaded with Diggs to hear him out before Diggs met with me, I'll bet Diggs would have done it. Diggs had been hanging around on the fringes of the mob for years. He probably never gave a thought to danger coming from Harold Talent."

Rodriguez nodded his head. "Okay. Talent goes to see Diggs before you get there. Diggs lets him in the back door of his hotel. They go up. Talent shoots Diggs to keep Diggs quiet and maybe get rid of you, too, for killing Diggs." He nodded again. "All right, I'll buy that. Now tell me who killed Norman Colquist?"

"I don't know."

"You sound like you don't want to know."

"I don't. Who the hell cares anyway? It's over." I paused to change the subject. "What about Shaeffer?"

"On indefinite suspension. Don't worry about him. He has his hands full. You're sure you don't want to be moved?"

"Yeah, I'm sure," I said and watched him leave.

Three evenings later, two men came out of the shadows at the end of the terrace and stood beside me.

One said, "Somebody to see you, Broder."

The night seemed suddenly colder.

They pushed my wheelchair to the ramp and down to the sidewalk and around the building to the parking lot. A Cadillac sat in lonely elegance in a dark corner of the lot. We went there.

A voice from the interior said, "Go have a smoke," and

the two men left us alone. A face moved closer to the open window of the car. The face chewed on a toothpick. "You know me, Broder?"

"No, but I can guess. You're Al Connor."

"You guess good," said Connor. He let his eyes wander the dark and empty grounds. "This is it for a lot of people, the last stop," he said. He looked back to me. "You screwed up a nice operation, Broder."

I said nothing to that.

Connor continued. "But you also did me a big favor, getting rid of Tommy Alvera and his top guns."

"I wasn't thinking about you at the time."

"Uh-huh." He took the toothpick out of his mouth. "That's straight enough. I didn't figure you had me on your mind. But a favor's a favor, Broder. I expect to run things like Manny did. He always looked out for people who did him favors. And he lived to be eighty-one years old and died in his own bed. I'd like to do that."

"What's that got to do with me?"

"I wanted to see you, see if you plan to make trouble for me like you did for Tommy Alvera."

"Alvera made his own trouble. He carried it around with him."

"That's right," he said. "Yes, that was Tommy, all right. You called it good, Broder. You have a good head on your shoulders."

"And that's where I'd like to keep it."

Connor laughed. In the semidarkness, his face was a white blur surrounding the black holes of his eyes. "I'm not looking to make trouble for you," he said. "I could do it easily enough, but I don't want any more killing. Things have to settle down. Last thing I need now are special prosecutors and task forces on crime and the rest of that shit." He returned the toothpick to his mouth. "You satisfied to call it all even, starting from here and now?"

I said, "I call it even all around."

He nodded, content. He put his hand out the window and slapped twice on the roof of his car, the sound carrying loudly over the quiet evening air. His two men appeared out of the shadows behind me and took their places in the front of the big car. Connor gave the convalescent home another look and said, "You okay here? Nobody giving you any trouble? Bills taken care of?"

"I'm getting along fine."

"All right," he said. "You ever need anything, you see me. Al Connor. You call me Al. Okay?"

"Right, Al."

"That's it. Big Al doesn't forget his friends. See you, Broder." He made a little movement and the power window went up, separating us, drawing the curtain on the corpse of Tommy Alvera.

Three weeks later, I was ambulatory enough to leave the convalescent home. I found a one-room apartment with bath and pullman kitchen, for which I paid winter rates. I spent most of my days in a health club gym, working out, swimming, taking the residual soreness out of my body with hot soaks in the whirlpool. The body came back—slowly, to be sure, but I could measure definite progress.

Margaret sent me a letter postmarked California, with no return address. She had a job, the kids were in school, and she was looking at several townhouses, for buying and settling down purposes. She had enough of Norm's money remaining for a down payment. She doubted she'd see anything that had been hers when she was married to Talent. Everything was tied up in litigation, because the government considered everything, even the house, as crime-sourced. She could never return to Florida. She could not expose the children to the sins of their father. The children weren't just important, they were everything. Of her past she had only them, and a few memories to cherish. Her letter sounded as though she had achieved a truce with life. I hoped so.

I spent nights alone in my room, pondering the one question over and over again. How had Norm's killer known where to find him? And the answer came back again and again, as it had, night after night, in the hospital and on the terrace of the convalescent home and in the silence of my darkened room. Again and again, until I had to find out for certain.

I got the address I needed from the list of visitors who had come to see me in the hospital. There were more than I might have expected. For their trouble they got to look at my unconscious self for sixty seconds and try to rouse me to wakefulness with kind words. Some had come from out of town. One had come from as far away as Mexico, leaving a name that I didn't recognize.

The plane put me down at the airport outside of Cancún, and I rode into the city in a Volkswagen taxi with a driver who wanted to give his limited English a workout and who kept looking in the rearview mirror for signs of my approval.

My destination was a hotel that was three stories high and had a fancy name in Spanish. The Sheraton would never have to worry about competition from it.

I paid my driver and went inside and walked to the desk. *"Señor Gomez, por favor."*

Gomez had gone out, probably to eat. He usually returned for *la siesta.* I gave the desk clerk five bucks American to keep his mouth shut.

I went back during siesta and went up to Gomez's room and knocked gently against the door. *"Momentito,"* said Gomez from within. I waited, and after the moment passed the door opened.

Gomez looked startled. His mouth opened, wordlessly, beneath his pencil-line mustache. The mustache made him look a little like a Latin gigolo from an old movie. It was dyed black, like his hair and eyebrows. An Anglo would take him

193

for a Mexican; a Mexican probably would think him Spanish. And why not? His grandmother had been Spanish, and he spoke the language as well as his sister.

"Hello, Norm," I said, and pushed him aside and walked past him into the room.

He shut the door and faced me. "What the hell?" he began. He seemed to have difficulty breathing. "How did you . . . ?"

"Dumb," I replied, "you coming to see me in the hospital. you had to leave your name and address to get in. You probably didn't know that until you got there, and then it was too late to back out without drawing attention to yourself."

I glanced around the room, not finding much to see. The bed, covers pulled back for siesta. A mirrored dresser with some personal stuff, two glasses, some bottled water, and a bottle of tequila on it. An upholstered chair next to a table on which sat a reading lamp. A small ottoman in front of the chair.

I sat down in the chair. "How did you know I was in the hospital?"

Norm Colquist went to the bed and sat on its edge. He was wearing a T-shirt and a pair of slacks, no shoes or socks. "Three-day-old Tampa paper off a cruise ship," he replied. "Big shoot-out at the beaches involving a well-known Tampa racketeer, a businessman, and a private eye. The paper didn't give you much of a chance of pulling through. I had to see for myself, had to let you know somebody was rooting for you."

"Big chance to take, just for that."

"Yeah." He looked down at the worn carpet on the floor, not at me. "I wore a hat and sunglasses and Mex clothes. I wanted to make sure it worked. I figured someday, no matter where I was, somebody would show up who knew me as Norm Colquist. I knew I'd never fool you or Margaret, of course, but it's the people you half know that can trip you up if you aren't careful." He paused, still looking downward. "I

194

also figured I owed you that much. I could get in and out of the hospital a lot easier than going to your funeral."

"Yeah. You did owe me that much. That and more."

"I didn't figure it would go so far," he pleaded.

"I got scars, Norm. The worst are those you can't see. Those are the ones inside, the kind you get when a friend lies to you and sets you up, knowing he's set you up. The scars where Alvera's bullets went in, you can see those, and they heal. It's the other ones, the ones inside, that don't heal. You don't forget those."

He had drawn the shades inside the room to shut out the glare of the afternoon sun. The old window air conditioner labored to cool the room.

He said, "It was Talent. All Talent." His hands, clasped together between his knees, wrestled with each other. "Talent got me into it."

"But it was your idea to bring me into it. That wouldn't have been Talent's idea. He didn't know me well enough. Not for what you wanted done."

"Paul," he began, "I'm sorry. I was desperate, crazy. You don't know what it's like, thinking about having a guy like Manny Diaz run you through a crematorium while you're still alive." He paused, his face gray in the uncertain light of the room.

"Want to tell me about it?"

He said, "The story I told you, about losing big, was true, only it happened nearly three years ago. Talent bailed me out."

"What did he want in return?"

"He had an idea that would make us both rich."

"Stealing from Manny Diaz. You made the biggest bet ever, Norm. You bet your life."

"We figured it was a sure thing. There was so goddamned much, we figured nobody would miss it. And they didn't. Talent combined the dirty money with legitimate income from the businesses. Then he set up phony businesses paralleling the real firms who supplied people like Diggs."

"If Diggs bought his soap from the ABC Soap Company, Talent would also write checks to the XYZ Soap Company, which didn't exist except on paper and which paid its income directly to Manny Diaz, income which became legitimate. Is that it?"

"Yes. But Harold saw he could carry it one step further, to phony companies that *he* collected from. That's where I came in. I set up the companies and bank accounts and cashed the checks that Talent wrote out of Diaz's money." He paused. "Want a drink of tequila?"

"Yes."

The bedsprings creaked as he rose from the bed and went to the dresser and put bottled water and tequila into his two glasses. He came back and handed one glass to me. "Sorry there's no scotch. It's expensive as hell here."

I took the glass and drank some of its contents and said, "And then you met Elinor Garcia."

"Yeah. Elinor. Fast-ass Elinor." He shook his head. "She hustled deals, mostly real estate. I was in the business of putting together package deals between businesses. Occasionally we worked together. We got friendly. She seemed interested."

"She had a nose for money, even if she couldn't see it," I said. "You knew she hustled. I'm surprised you went for it."

"Yeah. I knew how she earned her percentage, and because I knew I never thought she'd hustle me, for chrissake."

"She slept over, giving her a chance to go through papers you kept at home?"

"She found out somehow, and she wanted to score big off us. Either that or she'd blow the whole thing to Tommy Alvera. Said she had a cousin who knew Alvera. Talent said he'd take care of it. I didn't figure on murder. I figured he'd string her along or something."

"And in the event that he couldn't?" I asked. He made no

reply. He looked down at the floor, avoiding my eyes. I went on. "If she threatened to tell Alvera, you knew what it could come to."

He continued to look down at the floor. "Talent told me to go to the Bucs' game on Sunday afternoon and find a party afterward."

"He arranged a meeting with her at your place?" I asked, and he nodded. I said, "He withdrew twenty thou from one of his accounts on Friday. That was for Garcia?"

"Yeah." He stared into his glass for a long moment. "He knew me pretty well, I guess." His glance came back to me. "He meant the twenty thousand as a prop to hold up his story that he planned to buy her off. I've had plenty of time to think about it." He paused. "He planned to kill her from the beginning. He'd already told Margaret he had to go to Naples."

"What happened after you left the party?"

"I went back to my apartment. She was on the floor, dead. Talent had cleaned out the files I kept at home."

"Talent planned it to look like you had killed her."

"I guess so. I met him at the airport, as prearranged." He shrugged. He had lost weight since I last saw him. "Talent said I had two choices. I could keep my mouth shut and take the rap for Elinor's murder. Or I could tell the truth about him killing her because she had found out we were knocking down on Diaz. Of course, if I did that, and the state didn't fry me, Alvera would get me."

"But Talent had one other alternative," I suggested. "You disappearing and being killed by unknown mobsters for gambling debts was his idea?"

"Yeah. If I agreed, he'd send me money to set up a good life as Gomez. I was to let him know where I settled. He'd pay. He had to, in order to keep me away. If I returned and talked, the mob would kill him. Neither of us had much choice."

The air conditioner developed a momentary rattle, and somewhere close a door slammed. Otherwise, silence enveloped us.

He went on. "The story about me owing money was for the cops, to make my death look plausible. I called a few people from the airport, trying to raise money. They were people I knew wouldn't help and couldn't keep their mouths shut. It would go all over Tampa in a couple of days that Norm Colquist had lost his ass and was on the run from some bad guys."

"Who were the men who took you out of that barbershop?"

"Migrant workers I met in a bar. I told them it was a gag. Paid them each a hundred and bought their threads, best clothes they've ever owned. They weren't likely to read about it in the paper. They could hardly speak English, let alone read it. Besides, they were on their way back to Guatemala."

"And the body buried in your grave?"

He hesitated for a long moment. "Talent took care of that. I never knew." He paused. "A bum, maybe, a drifter, or an illegal immigrant. Shit, what difference does it make?"

"Not much, I guess. Not now. There had to be a corpse, badly mutilated, of course, so it would look like the mob had caught up to a deadbeat and it would be out of the question for your sister to have to go through the ordeal of identification. Your brother-in-law had to do that, as planned." I leaned forward in the chair. "After you cooked up the story about those gambling debts, you came to see me."

He avoided my eyes and said nothing.

I went on. "What you needed was some reality to back up that story about owing gamblers money. The people you called would put the word out on the street, but that wasn't enough. You needed somebody who would sweat for you, bleed for you if necessary. You called around until you found out where I was living. That wasn't too difficult, and in doing it you left a trail to me. Just in case nobody got the idea, you left my name and address in your car where the cops would find it. You knew the cops would come around to see me, and you knew I would keep my mouth shut tight. And the tighter I kept my mouth shut, the surer everybody would be that I was covering up for you and you really were in trouble. You knew I'd bleed for you, Norm. You counted on it."

He didn't want to talk about that. "How did you figure it out, Paul?" he asked instead. "I mean, about me not being dead?"

"Because nobody could have known where you were. Nobody, except one person." I stood up and looked down on him. "You knew, Norm. And that fit with the reason you lied about your gambling debts. You faked your death, and your partner in that fake, Talent, was the only one to identify your body."

I started for the door. He called my name. I turned at the door and faced my old friend, the brother of my ex-wife.

He said, "If Al Connor finds out I'm still alive, after what Talent and I did to him . . ." His voice trailed off.

"He'd hunt you down and kill you," I said.

"Jesus, Paul. I'm sorry I got you into this. I never thought it'd get this bad. I'm really sorry. But, Jesus, you can't tell anybody I'm still alive."

I stood for a long moment by the door. "The twenty thousand that Talent withdrew from the bank before he killed Garcia. He gave it to you?"

He nodded. "I got sixteen or so left. You want a split?"

I shook my head. "No," I said. "I don't even want the five hundred I gave you on the way to Ocala. You keep it. You'll need it. There won't be any money coming from Talent. Not now."

"You won't say anything about me being alive?"

"No. Your epitaph has already been written. Let's just keep it that way."

"Yeah. Thanks, Paul. You're a good friend. The goddam best."

"Don't kid yourself, pal. It's not for you. It's for your sister. She hasn't a dime to show for her eight years with Harold Talent. All she has is what her dead brother left her. That's clean money, because nobody but me can tie you into Talent's scheme. You come back and you'll have to talk, and then the money you left her goes to the government or to your lawyer, if you live long enough to need a lawyer. That money will buy a decent start in a new life for her and her kids, so you stay dead."

"Paul, wait. Stay and talk awhile. Have another drink."

I cut him off. "Goodbye, Norm."

"It was good once, Paul. You and me and Marg." He looked around the room as though seeing it for the first time. "Gone now. All gone, like it never happened."

I opened the door. "Sorry to have troubled you, *Señor* Gomez. You resemble someone I once knew, a long time ago. But he's dead now, dead and buried and forgotten. *Adios.*"

I went out of the room and down the stairs and across the tiny lobby and outside into the heat of the afternoon sun. He hadn't tried to come after me, and that was all right. When I walked away from Norm Colquist in that dingy hotel room, I put him and all of them in a small box and put the box up on a shelf in my mental attic. I could take the box down and look inside at the memory if I wanted to, but the box itself would stay out of sight and out of mind and out of the way of the new people I had yet to meet. Those new people would come along, and some of them would probably lie to me too. And some of them might shoot at me. Some could even love me, I supposed. New people: liars, shooters, lovers, losers.

200

If you have enjoyed this book and would like to receive details of other Walker mystery titles, please write to:

Mystery Editor
Walker and Company
720 Fifth Avenue
New York, NY 10019